Theodore F. Wolfe

A Literary Pilgrimage

Among the haunts of famous British authors

Theodore F. Wolfe

A Literary Pilgrimage
Among the haunts of famous British authors

ISBN/EAN: 9783337287634

Printed in Europe, USA, Canada, Australia, Japan

Cover: Foto ©Andreas Hilbeck / pixelio.de

More available books at **www.hansebooks.com**

A LITERARY PILGRIMAGE

AMONG THE HAUNTS OF FAMOUS BRITISH AUTHORS

BY THEODORE F. WOLFE
M.D. Ph.D.

AUTHOR OF LITERARY SHRINES ETC.

J. B. LIPPINCOTT COMPANY
PHILADELPHIA MDCCCXCVII

PREFACE

THE favor with which a few articles in the periodical press, similar to those herewith presented, have been received induces the hope that the present volume may prove acceptable. If some popular literary shrines which are inevitably included in the writer's personal itinerary are herein accorded but scant notice, it is for the reason that they have been already so oft described that portrayal of them is therefore purposely omitted from this account of a literary pilgrimage : even Stratford-on-Avon here for once escapes description. However, the initial paragraphs of these chapters lightly outline a series of literary rambles which the writer has found measurably complete and consecutive. The pilgrim is understood to make his start from London.

If these notes of his sojourns in the scenes hallowed by the presence of British authors or embalmed in their books shall prove pleasantly reminiscent to some who have fared to the same

Preface

shrines, or helpfully suggestive to others who contemplate such pilgrimage, then

> " not in vain
> He wore his sandal shoon and scallop-shell."

The writer is indebted to the publishers of the *Home Journal* for permission to reproduce on. or two articles which have appeared in that periodical.

T. F. W.

A LITERARY PILGRIMAGE

TENTH EDITION

CONTENTS

Contents

Contents

Contents

ILLUSTRATIONS

LITERARY HAMPSTEAD AND HIGHGATE

Haunt of Dickens—Steele—Pope—Keats—Baillie—Johnson—Hunt —Akenside—Shelley —Hogarth—Addison—Richardson—Gay— Besant— Du Maurier — Coleridge, etc.—Grave of George Eliot.

THE explorations which first brought re-nown to the immortal Pickwick were made among the uplands which border the val-ley of the Thames at the north of London : the illustrious creator of Pickwick loved to wander in the same region through the picturesque landscapes he made the scenes of many incidents of his fiction, and the literary prowler of to-day can hardly find a ramble more to his mind than that from the former home of Dickens or George Eliot by Regent's Park to Hampstead, and thence through the famous heath to Highgate. The way traverses storied ground and teems with his-toric associations, but these are, for us, lessened and subordinated by the appeal of memories of the famous authors who have loved and haunted this delightful region, and have imparted to it the tenderest charm. The acclivity of Hamp-stead has measurably resisted the encroachment of London, and has deflected the railroads with their disturbing tendencies, so that this old town probably retains more of its ancient character

than any other of the near suburbs, and some
of its quaint streets would scarcely be more
quiet if they lay a hundred miles away from the
metropolis. Off the highway by which we
ascend the hill, we find many evidences of antiquity, old streets lined by rows of plain and
sedate dwellings wearing an air of dignified
sobriety which is not of this century, and
which is in grateful contrast with the pert arti-
ficiality of the modern fabrics of the vicinage.
Many old houses are draped with ivy or
shrouded by trees of abundant foliage; some
are shut in by depressing brick walls, over which
float the perfumes of unseen flowers. A few
of the older streets lie in perpetual crepuscule,
being vaulted by gigantic elms and limes as
opaque as arches of masonry.

Along the slope of Haverstock hill, where
our ascent begins, we find the sometime homes
of Percival, Stanfield, Rowland Hill, and the
historian Palgrave. Near by is the cottage where
dwelt Mrs. Barbauld, and the Roslyn House,
where Sheridan, Pitt, Burke, and Fox were
guests of Loughborough. Here, too, formerly
stood the mansion where Steele entertained the
poet of the " Dunciad," with Garth and other
famed wits. On the hill-side a leafy lane leads
out of High Street to the picturesque church
of the parish, whose tower is a conspicuous

landmark. Within this fane we find, against the wall on the right of the chancel, the beautiful marble bust recently erected by American admirers "To the Ever-living Memory" of the author of "Lamia" and "Hyperion." Here, too, is the plain memorial tablet of the poetess Joanna Baillie, who lived in an unpretentious mansion lately standing in the neighborhood, where she was visited by Wordsworth, Rogers, and others of potential genius. In the thickly tenanted church-yard she sleeps with her sister near the graves of Incledon, Erskine, and the historian Mackintosh. Below the church, on the westering slope, lies embowered Frognall, once the home of Gay, where Dr. Johnson lived and wrote "The Vanity of Human Wishes" in the house where the gifted Nichol now resides with the author of "Ships that Pass in the Night" for a neighbor and with the home of Besant in view from his study. Near the summit of Hampstead stands a sober old edifice which was of yore the Upper Flask tavern, where the famous Kit-Kat Club held its summer *séances*, when such luminous spirits as Walpole, Prior, Dorset, Pope, Congreve, Swift, Steele, and Addison assembled here in the low-panelled rooms which we may still see, or beneath the old trees of the garden, and interchanged sallies of wit and fancy over their cakes and ale. To

A Literary Pilgrimage

this inn Lovelace brought the "Clarissa Harlowe" of Richardson's famed romance, and here
Steevens, the scholiast of Shakespeare, lived and
died.   Flask Walk, which leads out of the high
street among old houses and greeneries, brings
us to the shadowy Well Walk, with its overarching trees and with many living memories
masoned into its dead walls.   Here we see the
little remnant of the once famous well which
for a time made Hampstead a resort for the
fashionable and the suffering.   Among the
fancied invalids who once dwelt in Well Walk
was the spouse of Dr. Johnson.   Akenside,
Arbuthnot, and Mrs. Barbauld (editor of "Richardson's Correspondence") have sometime lived
in this same little street; here the mother of
Tennyson died, and here the sweet boy-poet
Keats lodged and wrote "Endymion."   At a
house still to be seen in the vicinage he was for
two years the guest of his friend Brown; here
he wrote "Hyperion," "St. Agnes," and the
"Ode to a Nightingale," and here he wasted in
mortal illness, being at last removed to Rome
only to die.   Under the limes of Well Walk is
a spot especially hallowed by the memory of
Keats: it was the object and limit of his walks
in his later months, and here was placed a seat
(which until lately was preserved and bore his
name), where he sat for hours at a time beneath

16

the whispering boughs, gazing, often through tears, upon the enchanting vista of wave-like woods and fields, the valley with its gleaming lakelets, and the farther slopes crowned by the spires of Highgate, which rise out of banks of foliage. The view is no less beautiful than when Keats's vision lingered lovingly upon it, although we must go into the open fields to behold it now.

If we bestir ourselves to reach the summit of the heath before the accustomed pall shall have settled down upon the great city, the exertion will be abundantly rewarded by the prospect that greets us as we overlook the abodes of eight millions of souls. Such a view is possible no-where else on earth : outspread before us lies the vast metropolis with its seven thousand miles of streets, while without and beyond this aggrega-tion of houses we behold an expanse of land-scape diversified with vale and hill, copse and field, village and park, extending for leagues in every direction and embracing portions of seven of England's populous shires. We see the great dome of St. Paul's and the tall towers of West-minster rising out of the mass of myriad roofs; the Crystal Palace glinting amid its green terraces ; across the city we behold the verdured slopes of Surrey and, farther away, the higher hills of Sussex ; our eyes follow the course of the Thames from imperial Windsor, whose battlements are misty in the distance of the western horizon, to its mouth at Gravesend; yonder at the right is Harrow, set on its classic hill-top, with its ancient church by which the boy Byron idled and dreamed; northward we see pretty Barnet, where "Oliver Twist" met the "Dodger;" nearer is romantic High-gate, and all around us lie the green slopes and leafy recesses of the heath. Through these strode the murderer Sykes of Dickens's tale, and from the higher parts of this common we may trace the way of his aimless flight from the pur-suing eyes of Nancy,—through Islington and Highgate to Hendon and Hatfield, and thence to the place of his miserable death at Rotherhithe. There are hours of delightful strolling amid the mazes of the picturesque heath, with its alterna-tions of heathered hills and flower-decked dales, its pretty pools, its braes of brambled gorse and pine, its tangle of countless paths. One will not wonder that it has been the resort of *littéra-teurs* from the time of Dryden till now: Pope, Goldsmith, and Johnson loved to ramble here; Hunt, Dickens, Collins, and Thackeray were fa-miliar with these shady paths; Nichol, Besant, James, and Du Maurier are now to be seen among the walkers on the heath. A worn path bearing to the right conducts to the turf-carpeted vale where, in a little cottage whose site is now occupied by the inn, Leigh Hunt lived for some years. Such guests as Lamb, Hazlitt, Coleridge, Hood, and Cornwall came to this humble home, and here Shelley met Keats, the "Adonais" of his elegy. Not far away lie the ponds of Pickwick's unwearied researches; and in another corner of the common we find an ancient tavern bowered with shrubbery, in whose garden Addison and Steele oft sipped their ale of a summer evening, and where is still cherished a portion of a tree planted by Hogarth. On an elevation of the heath stands "Jack Straw's Castle," believed to mark the place of encampment of that rebel chieftain with his mob of peasantry. It is a curious old structure, with wainscoted walls, and was especially favored by Dickens, who often dined here with Maclise and Forster and read to them his MSS. or counselled with them concerning his plots. Out on the heath near by was found the corpse of Sadlier the speculator, who, after bankrupting thousands of confiding dupes, committed suicide here; his career suggested to Dickens the Merdle and his complaint of "Little Dorrit." Among the embowered dwellings beyond West Heath we find that in which Chatham was self-immured, the cottage in which Mrs. Coventry Patmore—the Angel in the House—died, the place where Crabbe sojourned with Hoare.

This vicinage has been the delight of artists from the time of Gainsborough, and is still a favorite sketching ground : here lived Collins and Blake, and Constable dwelt not far away. The author of " Trilby," who has recently taken front rank in the literary profession, long had home and studio in a picturesque ivy-grown brick mansion of many angles and turrets, in a quiet street upon the other side of the hill ; here among his treasures of art he commenced a third book soon to be published.

The highway which leads north from Jack Straw's affords an exhilarating walk, with a superb prospect upon either hand, and brings us to the historic Spaniard's Inn, a pleasant wayside resort decked with vines and flowers, where pedestrians stop for refreshments. Dickens oft came to this place, and here we see the shady garden, with its tables and seats, where Mrs. Bardell held with her cronies the mild revel which was interrupted by the arrest of the widow for the costs in Bardell *vs.* Pickwick. The quiet of this ancient inn was disturbed one night by a fierce band of Gordon rioters, who rushed up the paths of the heath on their way to Mansfield's house, and stopped here to drink or destroy the contents of the inn-cellars,—an occurrence which is graphically described by Dickens in the looting of the Maypole Inn of

Willet, in "Barnaby Rudge." Next to the Spaniard's once lived Erskine, and among the grand beeches of Caen Wood we see the house of Mansfield, where the daughter of Mary Montagu was mistress, and where illustrious guests like Pope, Southey, and Coleridge were entertained.

A farther walk through the noble wood brings us to the delightful suburb of Highgate, where we now vainly seek the Arundel House where the great Bacon died and find only the site of the simple cottage where Marvell, the "British Aristides," lived and wrote. The last home of the author of "Ancient Mariner" is in a row of pleasant houses on a shady street called The Grove, a little way from the high street, which was in Coleridge's time the great Northern coach-road from London. The house is a neat brick structure of two stories, in which we may see the room where the poet lodged and where he breathed out his melancholy life. A pretty little patch of turf is in front of the dwelling, a larger garden, beloved by the poet, is at the back, and the trees which border the foot-walk were planted in his lifetime. To this cosy refuge he came to reside with his friends the Gilmans; here he was visited by Hunt, who once lodged in the next street, Lamb, Hazlitt, Wordsworth, Shelley, De Quincey, and others of like fame; and here, for nineteen years, "afflicted with manifold infirmities," he continued the struggle against a baneful habit, which ended only with his life. His grave was made not far away, in a portion of the church-yard which has since been overbuilt by a school, among whose crypt-like under-arches we find the tomb of stone, lying in pathetic and perpetual twilight, where the poet sleeps well without the lethean drug which ruined his life. On this hill lived "Copperfield" with Dora, and at its foot is the stone where Whittington sat and heard the bells recall him to London.

On the slope toward the city is the most beautiful of the London cemeteries, with a wealth of verdure and bloom. Within its hallowed shades lie the ashes of many whose memories are more fragrant than the flowers that deck their graves. In a beautiful spot which was beloved by the sweet singer in life we find the tomb of Parepa Rosa, tended by loving hands; not far away, among the mourning cypresses, lie Lyndhurst and the great Faraday. A plain tombstone erected by Dickens marks the sepulchre of his parents, and by it lies his daughter Dora, her gravestone bearing now, besides her simple epitaph prepared by her father, the name of the novelist himself and the names of two of his sons. Here, too, is the grave of Rossetti's young wife, whence his famous poems were exhumed. Among the many tombs of the enclosure, the one to which most pilgrims come is that of the immortal author of "Romola." On a verdant slope we find the spot where, upon a cold and stormy day which tested the affection of her friends, the mortal part of George Eliot was covered with flowers and lovingly laid beside the husband of her youth. Wreaths of flowers conceal the mound, and out of it rises a monument of gray granite bearing her name and years and the lines

> "Of those immortal dead who live again
> In minds made better by their presence."

From the terraces above her bed we look over the busy metropolis, astir with its myriad pulses of life and passion, while its rumble and din sound in our ears in a murmurous monotone. As we linger amid the lengthening shadows until the sunset glory fades out of the sky above the heath and the lights of London gleam mistily through the smoke, we rejoice that we find the tomb of George Eliot, not in the aisles of Westminster, where some would have laid her, but in this open place, where the winds sigh a requiem through the swaying boughs, the birds swirl and twitter in the free azure above, and the silent stars nightly watch over her grave.

BY SOUTHWARK AND
THAMES-SIDE TO CHELSEA

Chaucer – Shakespeare – Dickens – Walpole – Pepys – Eliot – Rossetti – Carlyle – Hunt – Gay – Smollett – Kingsley – Herbert – Dorset – Addison – Shaftesbury – Locke – Bolingbroke – Pope – Richardson, etc.

IF our way to Southwark be that of the pilgrims of Chaucer's time, by the London Bridge, we have on our right the dark reach of river where Lizzie Hexam was discovered in the opening of " Our Mutual Friend," rowing the boat of the bird of prey; on the right, too, we see the Iron Bridge where " Little Dorrit" dismissed young Chivery; and a few steps bring us to a scene of another of Dickens's romances, the landing-stairs at the end of London Bridge, where Nancy had the interview with " Oliver Twist's" friends which cost the outcast her life. Here, too, the boy Dickens used to await admission to the Marshalsea, often in company with the little servant of his father's family who figures in his fiction as the " orfling" of the Micawber household and the " Marchioness" of the Brass establishment in Bevis Marks. In the adjacent church of St. Saviour, part of which was standing when the Father of English poetry sojourned in the near Tabard inn, is the effigied tomb of the poet Gower, a friend of Chaucer;

24

here also lie buried Shakespeare's brother Edmund, an actor; Fletcher the dramatist, who lived close by; and Lawrence Fletcher, coparcener of Shakespeare in the Globe Theatre, which stood near at hand, on a portion of the site of the brewery which Dr. Johnson, executor of his friend Thrale, sold to Barclay and Perkins. The extensions of this establishment now cover the site of a church where Baxter preached, and the sepulchre of Cruden, author of the " Concordance." In near-by Zoar Street, Bunyan preached in a large chapel near the Falcon tavern, which was a resort of Shakespeare. Of the Tabard inn, whence Chaucer's Canterbury company set out, the pilgrim of to-day finds naught save the name on the sign of the new tavern which marks its site on Borough High Street; and the picturesque White Hart, which stood near by—an inn known to Shakespeare and mentioned in his dramas—where Jingle of " Pickwick," eloping with Miss Wardle, was overtaken and Sam Weller discovered, was not long ago degraded into a vulgar dram-shop. Near St. Thomas's Church in this neighborhood formerly stood the hospital in which Akenside was physician and Keats a student. A little farther along the High Street we come to a passage at the left leading into a paved yard which was the court of the Marshalsea, and the high wall at the right is believed to have been a part of the old prison where Dickens's father was confined in the rooms which the novelist assigns to William Dorrit, and where " Little Dorrit" was born and reared.   In this court the Dickens children played, and under yonder pump by the wall Pancks cooled his head on a memorable occasion.   Just beyond is St. George's Church, where " Little Dorrit" was baptized and married, with its vestry where she once slept with the register under her head; adjoining is the church-yard, once overlooked by the prison-windows of Dickens and Dorrit, where the disconsolate young Chivery expected to be untimely laid under a lugubrious epitaph.   Another block brings us to dingy Lant Street—"out of Hight Street, right side the way"—where the boy Dickens lived in the back attic of the same shabby house in which Bob Sawyer afterward lodged and gave the party to Pickwick.   Beyond the next turning stood King's Bench Prison, where Micawber was incarcerated by his stony-hearted creditors, and beyond this again we come to the tabernacle where Spurgeon preached.   Turning at the site of Micawber's prison, the Borough Road conducts us, by the sponging-house where Hook was confined, to the Christ Church of Newman Hall,—successor to Rowland Hill : it is a beautiful edifice, erected largely by contributions from America, its handsome tower being designed as a monument to Abraham Lincoln and marked by a memorial tablet. A little way southward, we find among the buildings of Lambeth Palace the library of which Green, the historian of the " English People," was long custodian, and the ancient room where Essex and the poet Lovelace were imprisoned.

Recrossing Father Thames and passing the oft-described shrines of Westminster we come to Millbank, the region into which Copperfield and Peggotty followed the wretched Martha and saved her from suicide. Out of Millbank Street, a few steps by a little thoroughfare bring us into the somnolent Smith Square in which stands the grotesque church of St. John, where Churchill once preached,—described in " Our Mutual Friend" as a " very hideous church with four towers, resembling some petrified monster on its back with its legs in the air." To this place came Charley Hexam and his school-master and Wrayburn, for here in front of the church, at a house near the corner, Lizzie Hexam—the best of all Dickens's women— lodged with Jenny Wren. It was a little house of two stories, and its dingy front room—the shop of the dolls' dress-maker—later was used as a cheap restaurant, where we once regaled ourselves with a dish of equivocal tea while we looked about us and recognized the half-door across which Wrayburn indolently leaned as he chatted with Lizzie, the seat in front of the wide window where Jenny sat at her work with her crutch leaning against the wall, the corner to which she consigned her " bad old child" in his drunken disgrace, the stairs which led to Lizzie's chamber,—objects all noted by the observant glance of Dickens as he peered for a moment through the door-way. Sauntering southward by Grosvenor Road, where Lizzie walked with her brother and Headstone, we have beside us on the left the river, glinting and shimmering in the morning sunlight and alive with every sort of craft that plies for trade or pleasure. It was along these curving reaches of the Thames that the merry parties of the olden time, destined like ourselves to Chelsea, used to row over the miles that then intervened between London and the ancient village, and here, too, Franklin, then a printer in Bartholomew Close, once swam the entire distance from Chelsea to Blackfriars Bridge. The way along which we are strolling then lay in the open country, with leafy lanes leading aside among groves and sun-flecked fields. But woods and fields have disappeared under compact masses of brick and mortar, and the quaint old suburb is linked to the city by continuous streets and structures. Contact has not altogether destroyed the distinctive features of the ancient suburb, and we know when our walk has brought us to its borders. Few of its thoroughfares retain the dreamful quiet of the olden time, few of its rows of sombre and dignified dwellings have wholly escaped the modern eruption of ornate and staring architecture; the old and the new are curiously blended, but enough of the former remains to remind us that Chelsea is olden and not modern, and to revive for us the winsome associations with which the place is permeated. The suggestion of worshipful antiquity is seen in sedate, ivy entwined mansions of dusky-hued brick, in carefully kept old trees which in their saplinghood knew Pepys, Johnson, or Smollett, in quaint inns whose homely comforts were enjoyed by illustrious *habitués* in the long ago.

Our stroll beyond the Grosvenor Road brings us to the famous "Chelsea Physick Garden," presented to the Apothecaries' Society by Sloane, the founder of the British Museum, who was a medical student here; it was to this garden that Polyphilus of the "Rambler" was going to see a new plant in flower when he was diverted by meeting the chancellor's coach. At the adjoining hospital dwelt the gifted Mrs. Somerville, whose husband was a physician there;

and the ancient mansion of dingy brick, in
which Walpole lived, and where Pope, Swift,
Gay, and Mary Wortley Montagu were guests,
is a portion of the infirmary,—the great drawing-room in which the brilliant company met
being a hospital ward. A little way northward,
by Sloane Street, we come to Hans Place, where,
at No. 25, the sweet poetess Letitia Landon
("L. E. L.") was born in a tiny two-storied
house; she attended school in a similar house of
the same row, where Miss Mitford and the
authoress of "Glenarvon" had before been
pupils. Along the river again we find beyond
the hospital a passage leading to the place of
Paradise Row, where, in a little brick house,
the witching Mancini was visited by Charles
II. and poetized by the brilliant Evremond.
Here, at the corner of Robinson's Lane, Pepys
visited Robarte in "the prettiest contrived
house" the diarist ever saw; not far away a
comfortable old inn occupies the site of the
dwelling of the historian Faulkner, in the
neighborhood where the essayist Mary Astell
—ridiculed by Swift, Addison, Steele, Smollett,
and Congreve—had her modest home. Robert
Walpole's later residence stood near Queen's
Road West, and its grounds sloped to the river
just below the Swan Tavern, near the bottom
of the lane now called Swan Walk. It was at

this river inn that Pepys "got affright" on being told of an eruption of the plague in Chelsea.

For a half-mile or so westward from the Swan, picturesque Cheyne Walk—beloved of the *literati*—stretches along the river-bank. Its many old houses, with their solemn-visaged fronts overlooking the river, their iron railings, dusky walls, tiled roofs, and curious dormer-windows, are impressive survivors of a past age. At No. 4, a substantial brick house of four stories, with battlemented roof and with oaken carvings in the rooms, are preserved some relics of George Eliot, for this was her last home, and here she breathed out her life in the same room where Maclise, friend of Carlyle and Dickens, had died just a decade before. No. 16, a spacious dwelling with curved front and finely wrought iron railing and gate-way, was the home of Rossetti for the twenty years preceding his death. With these panelled rooms, which he filled with quaint and beautiful objects of art, are associated most of the memories of the gifted poet and painter. The large lower room was his studio, where one of his last occupations was painting a replica of "Beata Beatrix," the portrait of his wife, whose tragic death darkened his life. Around the fireplace in this room a brilliant company held the nightly *séances* which a participant styles feasts of the gods. Through the passage at the side the famous zebu was conveyed, and reconveyed after his assault upon the poet in the garden. The rooms above were sometime tenanted by Meredith, Swinburne, and Rossetti's brother and biographer, who was also Whitman's editor and advocate. Later, the essayist Watts, to whom Rossetti dedicated his greatest work, resided here to cherish his friend. The garden, where Rossetti kept his odd pets and where neighbors remember to have seen him walking in paint-bedaubed attire for hours together, is now mostly covered by a school. At first, many luminaries of letters and art came to him here,—Jones, Millais, Hunt, Gosse, Browning, Whistler, Morris, Oliver Madox Brown, whose death elicited Rossetti's "Untimely Lost," and others like them ; later, when baneful narcotics had sadly changed his temperament, he dwelt in seclusion, exercising only in his garden and seeing such devoted friends as Watts, Knight, Hake, "The Manxman" Hall Caine, and the gifted sister, author of "Goblin Market," etc., who was pictured by Rossetti in his "Girlhood of Mary Virgin," and who lately died. In his study here he produced his best work ; here he revised the poems exhumed from his wife's grave and wrote "The Stream's Secret" and other parts of the volume which made his fame and occasioned the battle between the bards Buchanan and Swinburne; here he wrote the magnificent "Rose Mary," "White Ship," etc., and completed the series of sonnets which has been pronounced "in its class the greatest gift poetry has received since Shakespeare."

No. 18 was the famous coffee-house and barber-shop of Sloane's servant Salter,—called "Don Saltero" by Gay, Evremond, Steele, Smollett, and the other wits who frequented his place. On the Embankment by this Cheyne Walk we find the statue of Carlyle; behind it is the dull little lane of Cheyne Row, whose quiet Carlyle thought "hardly inferior to Craigenputtock," and here at No. 5, later 24, a plain three-storied house of sullied brick,—even more dingy than its neighbors,—the pessimistic sage lived, wrote, and scolded for half a century. All the wainscoted rooms are sombre and cheerless, but the memory-haunted study seems most depressing as we stand at Carlyle's hearth-stone and look upon the spot where he sat to write his many books. The garden was a pleasanter place, with bright flowers his wife planted, and the tree under which he loved to smoke and chat. Here Tennyson lounged with him, devoted to a long pipe and longer discourse; here Froude oft found him on the daily visits which enabled him to picture the seer, "warts and all;" here

Dickens, Maclise, and Hunt saw him at his best, and here the latter wrote "Jenny Kissed Me," —Jenny being Mrs. Carlyle. To Carlyle in this sombre home came Emerson, Ruskin, Tyndal, and a host of friends and disciples from all lands, and hither will come an endless procession of admirers, for many Carlyle belongings have been recovered, and the place is to be preserved as a memorial of the stern philosopher. Around the corner Hunt lived, in the curious little house Carlyle described, and here he studied and wrote in the upper front room. On the next block of the same street stood the home of Smollett, which was removed the year that Carlyle came to dwell in the vicinage. It was a spacious mansion which had been the Lawrence manor-house. Smollett wrote here "Count Fathom," "Clinker," and "Launcelot Greaves," and finished Hume's "England." Here Garrick, Johnson, Sterne, and other starry spirits were his guests, and here later lived the poet Gay and wrote "The Shepherd's Week," "Rural Sports," and part of his comedies. In the cellars of some of the houses at the top of Lawrence Street may be seen remains of the ovens of the once famous Chelsea china-factory, where Dr. Johnson wrought for some time vainly trying to master the art of china-making,—his pieces always cracking in the oven: a service of china presented to him by the factorymen here was preserved in Holland House. A tasteful Queen Anne mansion with beautiful interior decorations, not far from the Carlyle house, was a domicile of the poet and æsthete Oscar Wilde. In the picturesque rectory of St. Luke's, a few rods north from Cheyne Row, the author of " Hypatia" and his scarcely less famed brother Henry, of " Ravenshoe," lived as boys, their father being the incumbent of the parish. Henry Kingsley presents, in his " Hillyars and Burtons," charming sketches of Chelsea as it existed in his boyhood. Overlooking the river at the foot of the adjoining street, we find Chelsea Church, one of the most curious and interesting of London's many fanes, albeit partially disfigured by modern changes. In its pulpit Donne, the poet-divine, preached at the funeral of the mother of George Herbert; at its altar the dramatist Colman was married. Among its many monuments we find the mural tablet of Sir Thomas More, a marble slab with an inscription by himself which formerly described him as " harassing to thieves, murderers, and heretics." Here lie the ancestors of the poet Sidney, and in the little church-yard are the graves of Shadwell the laureate, who died just back of the church, of the publisher of " Junius," and of a brother of Fielding. Leading back from the river here is Church Street, on which dwelt Swift, Atterbury, and Arbuthnot, while Steele had a little house near by. The next street is named for Sir John Danvers, whose house was at the top of the little street: his wife was the mother of the poet Herbert, who dwelt here for a time and wrote some of his earlier poems; Donne and the amiable angler Izaak Walton were frequent guests of Herbert's mother in this place. The adjacent street marks the place of Beaufort House, the palatial residence of Sir Thomas More, where he was visited by his much-married monarch; where the learned and colloquial author of " Encomium Moriæ," Erasmus, was sometime an inmate; and where, decades later, Thomas Sackville, Earl Dorset, wrote the earliest English tragedy, " Gorboduc." A time-worn structure between King's Road and the Thames was once the home of the bewitching Nell Gwynne, and in later years " became (not inappropriately) a gin-temple," as Carlyle said: this old edifice was also sometime occupied by Addison. Back of King's Road we find the venerable Shaftesbury House,—in which the famous earl wrote " Characteristics," Locke began his " Essay," and Addison produced some of his Spectator papers,—long transformed into a workhouse, in the grounds of which we are shown the place of " Locke's yew," recently removed. The Old World's End Tavern, by Riley Street, was the notorious resort of Congreve's " Love for Love ;" the once ill-famed Cremorne Gardens, just beyond, were erst part of the estate of a granddaughter of William Penn, who was related to the Penns of Stoke-Pogis, where Gray wrote the " Elegy." A near-by little ivy-grown brick house, with wide windows in its front and an iron balcony upon its roof, was long the home of Turner, and in the upper room, through whose arched window he could look out upon the river, he died. From the water-edge here we see, upon the opposite shore, the old church where Blake was married and Bolingbroke was buried, and from whose vestry window Turner made his favorite sketches; near by is a portion of the ancient house where Bolingbroke was born and died, where he entertained such guests as Chesterfield, Swift, and Pope, and where the latter wrote part of the " Essay on Man." Beyond Chelsea we find at Fulham the spot where lived and died Richardson, who is said to have written " Clarissa Harlowe" here; and, near the river, the place of the home of Hook, and his mural tablet in the old church by which he lies, near the grave of the poet Vincent Bourne. Our ramble by Thames-side may be pleasantly prolonged through a region rife with the associations we esteem most precious. Our way lies among the sometime haunts of Cowley, Bulwer, Pepys, Thomson, Marryat, Pope, Hogarth, Tennyson, Fielding, "Junius," Garrick, and many another shining one. Some of lesser genius dwell now incarnate in this memory-haunted district by the river-side,—the radical Labouchère, living in Pope's famous villa, Stephens, and the author of " Aurora Floyd,"— but it is the memory of the mighty dead that impresses us as we saunter amid the scenes they loved and which inspired or witnessed the work for which the world gives them honor and homage; we find their accustomed resorts, the rural habitations where many of them dwelt and died, the dim church aisles or the turf-grown graves where they are laid at last in the dreamless sleep whose waking we may not know.

THE SCENE OF GRAY'S ELEGY

The Country Church-Yard – Tomb of Gray – Stoke-Pogis Church – Reverie and Reminiscence – Scenes of Milton – Waller – Porter – Coke – Denham.

OUR visit to the country church-yard where the ashes of Gray repose amid the scenes his muse immortalized is the culmination and the fitting end of a literary pilgrimage westward from London to Windsor and the nearer shrines of Thames-vale. Our way has led us to the sometime homes of Pope, Fielding, Shelley, Garrick, Burke, Richardson ; to the birthplaces of Waller and Gibbon, the graves of "Junius," Hogarth, Thomson, and Penn ; to the cottage where Jane Porter wrote her wondrous tales, and the ivy-grown church where Tennyson was married. Nearer the scene of the "Elegy" we visit other shrines : the Horton where Milton wrote his earlier works, "Masque of Comus," "Lycidas," "Arcades ;" the Hallbarn where Waller composed the panegyric to Cromwell, the "Congratulation," and other once famous poems ; the mansion where the Herschels studied and wrote. We have had the gray spire of Stoke-Pogis Church in view during this last day of our ramble. From the summit of the "Cooper's Hill" of Denham's best-known poem, from the battlements of Windsor and the windows of Eton, from the elm-shaded meads that border the Thames and the fields redolent of lime-trees and new-mown hay where we loitered, we have had tempting glimpses of that " ivy-mantled tower" that made us wish the winged hours more swift ; for we have purposely deferred our visit to that sacred spot so that the even-tide and the hour the curfew tolled " the knell of parting day" across this peaceful landscape may find us amid the old graves where " the rude forefathers of the hamlet sleep." As we approach through verdant lanes bordered by fields where the ploughman is yet at his toil and the herds feed among the buttercups, the abundant ivy upon the tower gleams in the light of the declining sun, and the " yew-tree's shade" falls far aslant upon the mouldering turf-heaps. The sequestered God's-acre, consecrated by the genius of Gray, lies in languorous solitude, far removed from the highway and within the precincts of a grand park once the possession of descendants of Penn. Just without the enclosure stands a cenotaph erected by John Penn, grandson of the founder of Pennsylvania ; it represents a sarcophagus and is ostensibly commemorative of Gray, but, as has been said, it " resembles nothing so much as a huge tea-caddy," and its inscription celebrates the builder more than the bard. Within the church-yard all is rest and peace; the strife and fever of life intrude not here; no sound of the busy world breaks in upon the hush that pervades this spot, and " all the air a solemn stillness holds." Something of the serenity which here pervades earth and sky steals into and uplifts the soul, and the demons of greed and passion are subdued and silenced as we stand above the tomb of Gray and realize all the imagery of the " Elegy." While our hearts are thrilling with the associations of the place and the hour, while the ashes of the tender poet rest at our feet and the objects that inspired the matchless poem surround us, we may hope to share in some measure the tenderer emotions to which the contemplation of this scene stirred his soul. As we ponder these objects, upon which his loving vision lingered, they seem strangely familiar; we feel that we have known them long and will love them alway.

One must visit this spot if he would appreciate the absolute fidelity to nature of the " Elegy :" its imagery is the exact reproduction of the scene lying about us, which is practically unchanged since that time so long ago when Gray drafted his poem here. Above us rises the square tower, mantled with ivy and surmounted by a tapering spire whose shadow now falls athwart the grave of the poet; here are the rugged elms with their foliage swaying in the summer breeze above the lowly graves; yonder by the church porch is the dark yew whose opaque shade covers the site of the poet's accustomed seat on the needle-carpeted sward; around us are scattered the mouldering heaps beneath which, "each in his narrow cell forever laid," sleep the rustic dead. Some of the humble mounds are unmarked by any token of memory or grief, but many bear the "frail memorials," often rude slabs of wood, which loving but unskilled hands have graven with "uncouth rhymes and shapeless sculpture," with the names and years of the unhonored dead, and "many a holy text that teach the rustic moralist to die." Some of these lowly graves hold the forefathers of families who, not content with the sequestered vale of life which sufficed for these simple folk, have sought on another shore largesses of fame or fortune unattainable here. Among the names "spelled by the unlettered muse" upon the stones around us we see those of Goddard, Perry, Gould, Cooper, Geer, and many others familiar to our American ears. The overarching glades of the woods which skirt the sacred precinct were the haunt of the "youth to fortune and to fame unknown;" the nodding beech, that "wreathes

its old fantastic roots so high" in the grove at
near-by Burnham, was his favorite tree, as it was
that of Gray; afar through the haze of a golden
after-glow we see the "antique towers" of
Eton, the stately brow of Windsor, with its
royal battlements, and nearer the wave of woods
and fields and all the dream-like beauty of the
landscape upon which the eyes of Gray so often
dwelt, a landscape that literally glimmers in the
fading light.

A tablet set by Penn in the chancel wall
beneath the mullioned window is inscribed,
"Opposite this stone, in the same tomb upon
which he so feelingly recorded his grief at the
loss of a beloved parent, are deposited the remains of Thomas Gray, author of the Elegy
written in a Country Church-yard." A few feet
distant is the tomb he erected for his mother,
which now conceals the ashes of the gentle
poet. It is of the plainest and simplest, a low
structure of brick, covered by a marble slab.
No "storied urn or animated bust" is needed to
perpetuate the name of him who made himself
immortal; even his name is not graven upon the
marble. We are come directly from the splen-
dors of the royal chapels of Windsor, where
costly sculpture, gilding, and superlative epitaphs mark the sepulchres of some who were
mediocre or mendicant of mind and virtue, and

we are, therefore, the more impressed by the fitting simplicity of the poet's tomb among the humble dead whose artless tale he told. At the grave of Gray, how tawdry seems the pomp of those kingly mausoleums, how mean some of the lives the bedizened monuments commemorate, of how little consequence that the world should know where such dust is hid from sight! At the grave of Gray, if anywhere the wide world round, we will correctly value the vanities, ambitions, and rewards of earth. Gray's desire to be buried here saved him from what some one has called the "misfortune of burial in Westminster." While the pilgrim vainly seeks in that national mausoleum the tombs of Shakespeare, Milton, Byron, Gray, Wordsworth, Thackeray, Coleridge, Eliot, and others of divine genius, and finds instead the graves of many sordid and impure, entombment there may be a misfortune. Happily the poet of the Elegy reposes in his church-yard, beside the beings he best loved, on the spot he frequented in life and hallowed by his genius, among those whose virtues he sang; here his grave perpetually emphasizes the sublime teachings of his verse and affords a most touching association. The only inscription upon the slab is the poet's tribute to his aunt, Mary Antrobus, and to "Dorothy Gray, the careful and tender mother of many

STOKE-POGIS CHURCH

we are, therefore, the more impressed by the
fitting simplicity of the ......'s tomb among the
humble dead who e artle.. ta'r he told. At
the grave of Gray, h w tawdry seem the pomp
of those kingly mausoleums, how mean some
of the lives the bedizened monuments commemor-
orate, of how little consequence that the world
should know where such dust is hid from sight!
At the grave of Gray, if anywhere the wide
world round, we will correctly value the vanities,
ambitions, and rewards of earth Gray's desire
to be buri..d l tre saved him t ..m what some
one has ca''e' r m. tortun ..... t. r'.l in
Westminster." W n .he pilgr. .. .. s
in that national maus .... (.e to. . .. ..
speare, Milton, Byron, Gray, W . . .th,
Thackerr , Coleridge, Eliot, and oth... .. divine p.... ..! finds instead the graves o . ry
sordi. ....nt there may be a
misfortune. H.., u .. p..t of the Elegy
reposes in his ch rch .. . . the beings he
best loved, .. the sp..t he .. que .ed in life and
hallowed by his genius, among those whose
virtues he sang; here his grave perpetually emphasizes the sublime teachings of his verse and
affords a most touching association. The only
inscription upon the slab is the poet's tribute to
his aunt, Mary Antrobus, and to "Dorothy
Gray, the careful and tender mother of many

children, of whom one alone had the misfortune to survive her." It has been our pleasure on a previous day to seek out amid the din of London the spot where, in a modest dwelling, this mother gave birth to the poet, and where she and Mary Antrobus sold laces to maintain the " many children."

Set upon a gentle eminence in the midst of this peaceful scene, the church has a picturesque beauty which harmonizes well with its environment. It is low and sombre, but age has given a dignity and grace which would make it attractive apart from its associations. Overrunning the walls, shrouding the crumbling battlements of the tower, clambering along the steep roofs, clinging to the highest gables, and festooning the stained windows, are masses of dark ivy, which conceal the inroads of time and impart to the whole structure a beauty that wins us completely. The tower is early English, the chancel is Norman, and the newer portions of the edifice were already old when Gray frequented the place. A path bordered by abundant roses leads from the gate-way of the enclosure to the quaint porch of timbers and the entrance to the church. Within, the light falls dimly at this hour upon the curious little galleries of the peasantry, the great pew of the Penns, the humbler place at the end of the south aisle where

A Literary Pilgrimage

Gray came to pray, the huge mural tablet and the burial vault where the son of William Penn and his family sleep in death. In the park close by is the palace of the Penns, and the mansion where Charles I. was imprisoned and where Coke wrote some of his Commentaries and entertained his queen. Not far distant is the house —now a fine abode—which Gray shared for some years with his mother and aunt, and where his bedroom and study may still be seen. Farther away are the Beaconsfield which furnished the title of the gifted author of " Lothair," and the old church where Burke and Waller await the resurrection.

In the twilight we hastily sketch Gray's " ivy-mantled tower," and then sit by his tomb gazing upon the fading landscape and recalling the life of this divine poet and the lines of the matchless poem which was drafted here and with exquisite care revised and polished year after year before it was given to the world. It may not be generally known that he discarded six stanzas from the original draft,—among them this, written as the fourth stanza :

" Hark, how the sacred calm that breathes around
  Bids every fierce, tumultuous passion cease ;
In still small accents whispering from the ground
  A grateful earnest of eternal peace ;"

Discarded Stanzas

this, from the reply of the "hoary-headed swain :"

> " Him have we seen the greenwood side along
>   While o'er the heath we hied, our labor done,
> Oft as the wood-lark piped her farewell song
>   With wistful eyes pursue the setting sun;"

and this, from the description of the poet's grave :

> " There scattered oft, the earliest of the year,
>   By hands unseen, are showers of violets found;
> The redbreast loves to build and warble there,
>   And little footsteps lightly print the ground."

We may judge what was the high standard of Gray, and what the transcending quality of the finished poem from which its author could, after years of deliberation, reject such stanzas. The Elegy is the expression in divinest poetry of the best conceptions of a noble soul upon the most serious topic on which human thought can dwell. No wonder that the world has literally learned by heart those precious lines; that they are the solace of the thoughtful and the bereft in every clime where mortals meditate on death; that the brave Wolfe, on the way to his triumphal death, should recite them in the darkness and declare he had rather be their author than the victor in the morrow's battle;

that the great Webster, on his death-bed, should beg to hear them, and die at last with their melody sounding in his ears.

As the glow fades out of the darkening sky, the birds in the leafy elms one by one cease their songs, "the lowing herds wind slowly o'er the lea" to distant folds, the "drowsy tinklings" grow fainter, the summer wind sighing among the trees dies with the day, and the scene which seemed still before is noiseless now. In this hush we are content to leave this deathless poet and the spot he loved. We gather ivy from the old wall and a spray from the boughs of his dreaming yew, and take our way back to the busy haunts of men.

DICKENSLAND: GAD'S HILL
AND ABOUT

Chaucer's Pilgrims—Falstaff—Dickens's Abode—Study—Grounds —Walks — Neighbors — Guests — Scenes of Tales — Cobham— Rochester—Pip's Church-Yard—Satis House, etc.

"TO go to Gad's Hill," said Dickens, in a note of invitation, "you leave Charing Cross at nine o'clock by North Kent Railway for Higham." Guided by these directions and equipped with a letter from Dickens's son, we find ourselves gliding eastward among the chimneys of London and, a little later, emerging into the fields of Kent,—Jingle's region of "apples, cherries, hops, and women." The Thames is on our left; we pass many river-towns,—Dartford where Wat Tyler lived, Gravesend where Pocahontas died,—but most of our way is through the open country, where we have glimpses of fields, parks, and leafy lanes, with here and there picturesque camps of gypsies or of peripatetic rascals "goin' a-hoppin'." From wretched Higham a walk of half an hour among orchards and between hedges of wild-rose and honeysuckle brings us to the hill which Shakespeare and Dickens have made classic ground, and soon we see, above the tree-tops, the glittering vane which surmounted the home of the world's greatest novelist. The name Gad's (vagabond's) Hill is a survival of the time when the depredations of highwaymen upon "pilgrims going to Canterbury with rich offerings and traders riding to London with fat purses" gave to this spot the ill repute it had in Shakespeare's day: it was here he located Falstaff's great exploit. The tuft of evergreens which crowns the hill about Dickens's retreat is the remnant of thick woods once closely bordering the highway, in which the "men in buckram" lay concealed, and the robbery of the franklin was committed in front of the spot where the Dickens house stands. By this road passed Chaucer, who had property near by, gathering from the pilgrims his "Canterbury Tales." In all time to come the great master of romance who came here to live and die will be worthily associated with Shakespeare and Chaucer in the renown of Gad's Hill. In becoming possessor of this place, Dickens realized a dream of his boyhood and an ambition of his life. In one of his travellers' sketches he introduces a "queer small boy" (himself) gazing at Gad's Hill House and predicting his future ownership, which the author finds annoying "because it happens to be *my* house and I believe what he said was true." When at last the place was for sale, Dickens did not wait to examine it; he never was inside

Gad's Hill House

the house until he went to direct its repair.
Eighteen hundred pounds was the price; a
thousand more were expended for enlargement
of the grounds and alterations of the house,
which, despite his declaration that he had
"stuck bits upon it in all manner of ways,"
did not greatly change it from what it was when
it became the goal of his childish aspirations.
At first it was his summer residence merely,—
his wife came with him the first summer,—but
three years later he sold Tavistock House, and
Gad's Hill was thenceforth his home. From
the bustle and din of the city he returned to the
haunts of his boyhood to find restful quiet and
time for leisurely work among these "blessed
woods and fields" which had ever held his
heart. For nine years after the death of Dickens Gad's Hill was occupied by his oldest son;
its ownership has since twice or thrice changed.

Its elevated site and commanding view render
it one of the most conspicuous, as it is one of
the most lovely, spots in Kent. The mansion
is an unpretentious, old-fashioned, two-storied
structure of fourteen rooms. Its brick walls are
surmounted by Mansard roofs above which rises
a bell-turret; a pillared portico, where Dickens
sat with his family on summer evenings, shades
the front entrance; wide bay-windows project
upon either side; flowers and vines clamber

upon the walls, and a delightfully home-like air pervades the place. It seems withal a modest seat for one who left half a million dollars at his death. At the right of the entrance-hall we see Dickens's library and study, a cosy room shown in the picture of " The Empty Chair :" here are shelves which held his books ; the panels he decorated with counterfeit book-backs ; the nook where perched the mounted remains of his raven, the " Grip" of " Barnaby Rudge." By this bay-window, whence he could look across the lawn to the cedars beyond the highway, stood his chair and the desk where he wrote many of the works by which the world will know him alway. Behind the study was his billiard-room, and upon the opposite side of the hall the parlor, with the dining-room adjoining it at the back, both bedecked with the many mirrors which delighted the master. Opening out of these rooms is a conservatory, paid for out of "the golden shower from America" and completed but a few days before Dickens's death, holding yet the ferns he tended. The dining-room was the scene of much of that emphatic hospitality which it pleased the novelist to dispense, his exuberant spirits making him the leader in all the jollity and conviviality of the board. Here he compounded for bibulous guests his famous " cider-cup of Gad's Hill," and at the same table he was stricken with death ; on a couch beneath yonder window, the one nearest the hall, he died on the anniversary of the railway accident which so frightfully imperilled his life. From this window we look out upon a lawn decked with shrubbery and see across undulating cornfields his beloved Cobham. From the parquetted hall, stairs lead to the modest chambers,—that of Dickens being above the drawing-room. He lined the stairway with prints of Hogarth's works, and declared he never came down the stairs without pausing to wonder at the sagacity and skill which had produced the masterful pictures of human life. The house is invested with roses, and parterres of the red geraniums which the master loved are ranged upon every side. It was some fresh manifestation of his passion for these flowers that elicited from his daughter the averment, " Papa, I think when you are an angel your wings will be made of looking-glasses and your crown of scarlet geraniums." Beneath a rose-tree not far from the window where Dickens died, a bed blooming with blue lobelia holds the tiny grave of " Dick" and the tender memorial of the novelist to that " Best of Birds." The row of gleaming limes which shadow the porch was planted by Dickens's own hands. The pedestal of the sundial upon

the lawn is a massive balustrade of the old stone
bridge at near-by Rochester, which little David
Copperfield crossed "foot-sore and weary" on
his way to his aunt, and from which Pickwick
contemplated the castle-ruin, the cathedral, the
peaceful Medway. At the left of the mansion
are the carriage-house and the school-room of
Dickens's sons. In another portion of the
grounds are his tennis-court and the bowling-
green which he prepared, where he became a
skilful and tireless player. The broad meadow
beyond the lawn was a later purchase, and the
many limes which beautify it were rooted by
Dickens. Here numerous cricket matches were
played, and he would watch the players or keep
the score "the whole day long." It was in
this meadow that he rehearsed his readings, and
his talking, laughing, weeping, and gesticulating
here "all to himself" excited among his neighbors suspicion of his insanity. From the front
lawn a tunnel constructed by Dickens passes
beneath the highway to "The Wilderness," a
thickly wooded shrubbery, where magnificent
cedars uprear their venerable forms and many
sombre firs, survivors of the forest which erst
covered the countryside, cluster upon the hill-
top. Here Dickens's favorite dog, the "Linda"
of his letters, lies buried. Amid the leafy seclusion of this retreat, and upon the very spot

where Falstaff was routed by Hal and Poins
("the eleven men in buckram"), Dickens
erected the chalet sent to him in pieces by
Fechter, the upper room of which—up among
the quivering boughs, where "birds and butter-
flies fly in and out, and green branches shoot in
at the windows"—Dickens lined with mirrors
and used as his study in summer. Of the work
produced at Gad's Hill—"Two Cities," "Uncommercial Traveller," "Mutual Friend," "Edwin Drood," and many tales and sketches of "All
the Year Round"—much was written in this
leaf-environed nook; here the master wrought
through the golden hours of his last day of con-
scious life, here he wrote his last paragraph and
at the close of that June day let fall his pen,
never to take it up again. From the place of the
chalet we behold the view which delighted the
heart of Dickens,—his desk was so placed that
his eyes would rest upon this view whenever he
raised them from his work,—the fields of waving
corn, the green expanse of meadows, the sail-
dotted river.

Many friends came to Dickens in this pleasant
Kentish home,—Forster, Maclise, Reade, Ma-
cready, Leech, Collins, Yates, Hans Christian
Andersen, Mr. and Mrs. Fields, Longfellow and
his daughters, Fechter and his wife: some of
them were guests here for many days together.

A Literary Pilgrimage

The master was the most genial of hosts, apparently the happiest of men, with the hearty laugh which Montaigne says never comes from a bad heart. After the morning task in library or chalet he gave the rest of the day to exercise and recreation, often at games with his guests in the grounds, but taking daily in rain or shine the long walks which made his lithe figure and rapid gait familiar to all the cottagers and field-laborers of the countryside. It is pleasant to hear the loving testimony of these simple folk —many of them descendants of the "men of Kent" who followed the standard of Wat Tyler from Blackheath to London—concerning Dickens's uniform kindness, his helpful generosity, his scrupulous regard of the rights of inferiors, the traits which won their hearts. One rustic neighbor declares, "Dickens was a main good man, sir : it was a sorry day for the neighborhood when he was taken away." Near the gate of Gad's Hill House is a wayside inn, the "Sir John Falstaff," which for more than two centuries has stood for remembrance of that worthy's exploit at this place. Its weather-worn sign bears portraits of Falstaff and Prince Hal and a picture of the "Merry Wives of Windsor" putting Falstaff into the basket. The name of a son of the recent keeper of this hostelry, Edward Trood, doubtless suggested the title of the

Scenes of Great Expectations

" Mystery" which must, alas! remain a mystery evermore.

From the inn a lane leads to a sightly summit surmounted by a monument which Dickens called "Andersen's Monument," because it was the resort of that illustrious author while a guest at Gad's Hill. Its far-reaching prospect is indeed alluring : on every hand vast, wave-like expanses of forest and orchard, moor and mead, sweep away to the horizon, while north-ward, beyond great cornfields and market-gardens, we see twenty miles of the Thames—" stealing steadily away to the ocean, like a man's life" —bordered here by a wilderness of low-lying marsh. A walk beloved of Dickens brings us to one of his favorite haunts,—a dreary church-yard on the margin of this marsh. It lies in the dismal, ague-haunted "hundred of Loo," a peninsula between the Thames and the Medway having a broad hem of desolate fens along the river-banks—a weird, little known region, whose ancient reputation was unsavory. A wooden finger on a post directs us to Cooling,—Dickens makes Pip say that this direction was never ac-cepted, no one ever came,—a forlorn hamlet which straggles about the ruins of Cooling Cas-tle. This was an ancient seat of the Cobhams ; through a Cobham heiress it passed to Oldcastle, leader of the Lollards, who shut himself up here and was dragged hence to martyrdom. It is noteworthy that this Oldcastle has been thought to be the original of Falstaff, the hero of Gad's Hill. Of the stronghold little remains save the machicolated gate-way, flanked with ponderous round towers bearing quaint inscriptions. The water of the moat is green and stagnant, suggesting frogs and rheumatism, and the space it encloses is occupied by the cottage of a farmer. The forge and cottage of Joe Gargery are not found in the wretched village,—indeed, we should be sorry to find that splendid fellow and the good Betty so poorly housed,—but beyond the narrow street and at the verge of the marshes we come to a low, quaint, square-towered old church, which rises from a wind-swept, nettle-grown church-yard, the scene of the opening chapter of "Great Expectations." Yonder mound, whose gravestone is inscribed to George Comfort, "Also Sarah, Wife of the Above," stands for the tomb of Pip's parents ; and sunken in the grass at our feet is the row of little grave-stones whose curious shape led Pip to believe that his little brothers (whose graves they marked) "had been born on their backs, with their hands in their trousers pockets, and had never taken them out in this stage of existence." Over this low wall which divides God's-acre from the marshes the convict climbed, and we, standing upon it, look across the scene of his chase and capture, which Pip witnessed from Joe's back. On this sombre autumn afternoon of our visit the landscape is startlingly like that the terrified boy beheld : we see the same far-stretching waste of marshes, the intersecting dikes, the low, leaden line of the river beyond, dark mists hanging heavy over all, while the chill wind blows in our faces from its "savage lair" in the sea. Upon yonder flat tombstone in the far corner of the church-yard Dickens sat and lunched with Fields when he last walked to this place. Hidden now in the mists, but not far distant, and reached by a foot-path from the road to Chalk, is a dirty and dilapidated Thames-side inn, whose creaking sign-board reads, " Ship and Lobster :" this is The Ship of " Great Expectations," where Pip and his party slept the night preceding their attempt to put Magwich on the steamer, and the open river below the little causeway is the scene of their mischance and the transport's recapture.

The walk which Dickens most enjoyed—the one which was his last before he died—was to and around Cobham, the seat of his friend Darnley. We follow the way once so familiar to his feet, through the noble park which the Pickwick Club found "so thoroughly delightful," on a June afternoon, by the stately old hall where lately stood Dickens's chalet, and farther, through majestic forest and open glade, to the place whence Pickwick—overcome by cold punch—was wheeled to the pound. Skirting the park on our return, we come to Cobham village and the neat Leather Bottle Inn to which the lovelorn Tupman retired to conceal his woe after his discomfiture at Manor Farm, and where Dickens himself, rambling in the neighborhood with Forster, lodged in 1841. Here is the little church-yard where Pickwick walked with Tupman and persuaded him to return to the world, and hard by the cottage of Bill Stumps, before which Pickwick made the immortal discovery which was " the pride of his friends and the envy of every antiquarian in this or any other country." Another favorite walk of Dickens conducts us, past a quaint, rambling mansion of dingy brick which served as the model for Satis House of " Great Expectations," to Rochester, the Cloisterham of " Edwin Drood." Here we find the Bull Inn,—" good house, nice beds,"—where the Pickwick Club lodged, in rooms 13 and 19, and the ballroom, where Tupman and Jingle (the latter in Winkle's coat) danced with the widow and enraged little Slammer ; the Watt's Charity of " The Uncommercial Traveller ;" the picturesque castle-ruin which Dickens frequented and has so charmingly described. Here, too, is the gray old cathedral he loved, which appears in many of his tales, from Jingle's piquant account of it in "Pickwick" to that touching description of this ancient fane in the last lines of the master, written within sound of its bells and but a few hours before his death.

This region of sunny Kent, the scene of his earliest and latest years, may fitly be called The Land of Dickens, so intimately is it associated with his life and work. Here at near-by Chatham (whence he used to come to gaze longingly at Gad's Hill House), in a whitewashed cottage on Ordnance Place, he lived as a child; at yonder village of Chalk he spent his honeymoon, its expenses being defrayed by the sale of the first numbers of " Pickwick ;" here were the habitual resorts of his holiday leisure; here was his latest home ; here he died, and here he desired to be buried. This district was no less the life-haunt and home of his imagination and genius. The scenes of his most effective romances are laid here; into the fabric of many a tale and sketch his fancy has woven the familiar features of town and hamlet, field and forest, marsh and river, of the region he knew and loved so well; here his first tale opens, here his last tale ends.

SOME HAUNTS OF BYRON

OF the places in and about great London which were associated with the brief life of Byron, the rage for improvement which holds nothing sacred has spared a few, and the quest for Byron-haunts is still fairly rewarded. Holles Street, where he was born, has not long been resigned to trade: we have known it as a somnolent little street whose grateful quiet—reached by a step from the tumult of De Quincey's "stony-hearted step-mother"—made it seem like a placid pool beside a riotous torrent. It is scarce a furlong in length, and from the shade of Cavendish Square at its extremity we could look, between bordering rows of modest dwellings, to the square where Ralph Nickleby lived and Mary Wortley Montagu died. At our right, a little way down the street, stood a small, plain, two-storied house of dingy brick, where the poet's mother lodged in the upper front room at the time of his birth. This dwelling was No. 16, later 24, and has now given place to a shop. An unpretentious tenement near Sloane Square was Byron's home during his pupilage with Dr. Glennie.

London Homes

In the house No. 8 St. James Street, nearly opposite the place where Gibbon died, Byron had for some years a suite of rooms. Here he was convenient to Almack's aristocratic ballrooms and St. James Theatre, and was in the then, as it is now, centre of fashionable club-life. His residence here began when he came to London to publish " Bards and Reviewers," was resumed upon his return from the Levantine tour, and continued during the publication of the early cantos of " Childe Harold" and other poems written on that tour. In these rooms " Corsair," " The Giaour," and " Bride of Abydos" were written, the latter in a single night and with one quill. The last year of Byron's residence here was the period of his highest popularity, when he was the especial pet of London society queens, one of whom—who later wrote a book to defame him—was recognized in bifurcated masculine garb in these chambers. On the same street is the home of White's Club, the Bays' of " Pendennis," of which the present Lord Byron is a member, and on the site of the Carlton Club, Pall Mall, stood the Star and Garter tavern, where, in room No. 7 at the right on the first floor, the poet's predecessor killed his neighbor Chaworth, grand-uncle of Byron's " star of Annesley." Adjoining the Academy of Arts in Piccadilly is that " college of bachelors," the Albany apartment house where Dickens lodged " Fascination" Fledgeby and laid the scene of his flagellation by Lammle and the dressing of his wounds with pepper by Jenny Wren. Here the handsome suite A 2 was the abode of Byron for the year or so preceding his hapless marriage, and here " Lara" and " Hebrew Melodies" were written. The poet had passed the zenith of the social horizon, and the " Byron-madness" was waning, when he came to the Albany ; still, the visits of fair admirers were vouchsafed him in these rooms. It was here that the girl whose story Guiccioli adduces as evidence of Byron's virtuous self-denial came to him for counsel. If the partiality of his mistress has unduly praised his conduct at this time, it is a thousandfold outweighed by the bitterness of another narrative—happily discredited, if not disproven—which indicates this same period as being that of the beginning of a *liaison* with his sister. To these rooms Moore was a daily visitant, and Canning then lodged on the second floor adjoining the suite E 1, where Macaulay wrote the " History of England" and many essays. Byron's last abode in London was a stately house in Piccadilly, opposite Green Park and not far from the then London sojourn of Scott. Byron's dwelling, now No. 139, belonged to the Duchess of Devon, and was known as 13 Piccadilly Terrace. To this elegant home he brought his bride after the " treacle-moon," and here passed the remainder of their brief period of cohabitation. Here " The Siege of Corinth," " Parisina," and many minor poems were penned, the MS. of some being in the handwriting of his wife. Here Augusta Leigh was a guest warmly welcomed by Lady Byron, despite her alleged knowledge of the " shocking misconduct" of Byron and his sister in this house. Here Ada, " sole daughter of his house and heart," was born, and from here, a few weeks later, his wife went forth, never to see him again. Some letters came from her to this home,—playful notes to Byron inviting him to follow her, affectionate epistles to the sister, then a final letter announcing her determination never to return. In the ten months during which Byron occupied this house it was nine times in possession of bailiffs on account of his debts. It has since been refaced and repaired, but the original rooms remain. Hamilton Place now leads from it to Hamilton Gardens, where stands a beautiful statue of Byron. To the mansion of Sir Edward Knatchbull, No. 25 Great George Street, a site now occupied by the Institute of Engineers, the corpse of Byron was brought upon its arrival from Greece ; and here in the great parlors, but a few steps from the spot where the remains of Sheridan had lain eight years before, Byron's body lay in state while his friends vainly sought sepulture for it in Westminster.

At No. 50 Albemarle Street, Piccadilly, not far from the Albany, is the establishment of John Murray, whose predecessor, John Murray II., published "Childe Harold" and all Byron's subsequent poems to the earlier cantos of "Don Juan." At this house the poet was a frequent and familiar lounger. Here, in a cosy drawing-room which is handsomely furnished and embellished, Murray used to hold a literary court, and here Byron first shook hands with the "great Wizard of the North" and met Moore, Canning, Southey, Gifford, and other *littérateurs*. Scott afterward wrote, "Byron and I met for an hour or two daily in Murray's drawing-room, and found much to say to each other." During his residence in London, Byron was customarily one of the coterie of authors—facetiously called the "four o'clock club"—which daily assembled in this room. The *séances* were frequented at one time or another by most of the stars of English letters, embracing, besides those above named, Campbell, Hallam, Crabbe, Lockhart, Disraeli, Irving, George Ticknor, etc. We find the room little changed since their time. Original portraits of that brilliant company look down from the walls of the room they haunted in life, and the visitor thrills with the thought that in some subtile sense their presence pervades it still. In this room Ada Byron, kept in ignorance of her father until womanhood, first saw his handwriting, and in yonder fireplace beneath his portrait, four days after intelligence of his death had reached London, the manuscript of his much-discussed "Memoirs" was burned at the desire of Lady Byron and in the presence of Moore and Byron's executor, Hobhouse, who had witnessed his hapless marriage. Until the death of Byron his relations with Murray were most cordial, and the present John Murray IV., grandson of Byron's publisher, possesses numerous letters of the poet, some of which were used in Moore's "Life." Perhaps most interesting of Byron's many rhyming epistles is the one commencing,—

> "My dear Mr. Murray,
> You're in a blanked hurry
> To set up this ultimate canto,"

which announces the final completion of "Childe Harold." Among many mementos of Byron cherished in this famous room are the original MSS. of "Bards and Reviewers" and of most of his later poems. With them are other priceless MSS. of Scott, Swift, Gray, Southey,

A Literary Pilgrimage

Livingstone, Irving, Motley, etc. The Murray
III. who used to show us these treasures with
reverent pride, and who could boast that he
had known Byron, Scott, and Goethe, died not
long ago. When we ask for the Bible popularly
believed to have been given to Murray by Byron
with a line so altered as to read " now Barabbas
was a *publisher*," we are told this joke was
Campbell's and was upon another publisher than
Murray. Byron's signet-ring has passed to the
possession of Pierre Barlow, Esq., of New York.
Littérateurs still come to " Murray's den,"
though not so often as in the time when clubs
were less popular : among those who may sometimes be met here are Argyll, Knight, Layard,
Dufferin, Temple, Francis Darwin, etc. Mur-
rays' was the home of the Review—"whose
mission in life is to hang, draw, and *Quarterly*,"
as one victim avers—to which came Charlotte
Brontë's burly Irish uncle with his shillalah in
search of the harsh reviewer of "Jane Eyre,"
and haunted the place until he was turned away.

A most delightful outing is the jaunt from
Byron's London haunts, past Kensal Green,
where we find the precious graves in which
sleep Thackeray, Motley, Cunningham, Jame-
son, Hood, Hunt, Sydney Smith, and Mrs.
Hawthorne,—the latter beneath ivy from her
Wayside home and periwinkle from her hus-

band's tomb on the piny hill-top at Concord,—
to Harrow, the "Ida" of Byron's verse. Here
is the ancient school of which Sheridan, Peel,
Perceval, Trollope, and others famous in letters
or politics were inmates; where Byron was for
years "a troublesome and mischievous pupil"
and made the acquaintance of Clare, Dorset,
and others to whom some of his poems are
addressed, and of Wildman who rescued his
Newstead from ruin: the present Byron and
the son of Ada Byron were also Harrow boys.
Here may be seen some of the poet's worn and
scribbled books; his name graven by him upon
a panel of the oldest building; the Peachie
tombstone—protected now by iron bars—which
was his evening resort, where some of his
stanzas were composed, and whence he beheld
a landscape of enchanting beauty. Near this
beloved spot, where Byron once desired to be
entombed, sleeps a sinless child of sin, his
daughter Allegra, born of Mrs. Shelley's sister.
At Harrow, Byron repaid help upon his exer-
cises by fighting for his assistant; his successes
here were mainly pugilistic, but his battles were
often those of younger and weaker boys, and
the spot where he fought the tyrants of the
school is pointed out with interest and pride.

In Notts, *en route* to Newstead, we lodge in
an old mansion alleged to have been the abode

of the poet in his school-vacations; we have the high authority of the landlord for the conviction that we occupy the room and the very bed oft used by Byron; but the credulity even of a pilgrim has a limit, and the agility of the fleas that now inhabit the bed forbids belief that they too are relics of the poet. Better authenticated are the Byron relics of a local society, among which are the boot-trees certified by his bootmaker to be those upon which the poet's boots were fitted. They are of interest as demonstrating that the asymmetry of his feet was much less than has been believed; one foot was shorter than its fellow, and the ankle was weak, but not deformed.

From Nottingham a winsome way along a smiling vale, with billowy hills swelling upon either hand, conducts us to the village of Hucknall. By its market-place an ancient church-tower rises from a grave-strewn enclosure; we enter the fane through a porch of ponderous timbers, and, traversing the dim aisle, approach the chancel and find there the tomb of Childe Harold. A slab of blue marble, sent by the King of Greece and bearing the word Byron, is set in the pavement to mark the spot where, after the throes of his passion-tossed life, Byron lies among his kindred in " the dreamless sleep that lulls the dead." One who, as a lad, en-

Tomb of Childe Harold

tered the vault at the burial of Ada Byron, indicates for us its size upon the pavement and the position of the coffins; Byron, in a coffin covered with velvet and resting upon benches of stone, lies between his mother and the "sole daughter of his house and heart;" at his feet a receptacle contains his heart and brain. His valet and the Little White Lady of Irving's narrative sleep in the yard near by. A marble tablet on the church wall describes Byron as the "Author of Childe Harold's Pilgrimage;" this was erected by his sister, and near it we saw a chaplet of faded laurel placed years ago by our "Bard of the Sierras." Byron's tomb has never been a popular shrine, but such Americans as Irving, Hawthorne, Halleck, Ludlow, Joaquin Miller, and William Winter have been reverent pilgrims. Once Byron's "Italian enchantress," la Guiccioli, was found weeping here and kissing the pavement which covers the lover of her youth.

Above Hucknall the ancestral domain of the Byrons lies upon the right, while upon the other hand extend the broad lands which were the heritage of Mary Ann Chaworth, Byron's "star of Annesley." From the boundary of the estates, where the poet sometimes met his youthful love, a stroll across a landscape parquetted with grain-field gold and meadow emerald brings us to the ancient seat of the time-honored race of which the maiden of Byron's " Dream"— the " Mary" of many poems—was the " last solitary scion left." It is now the property of her great-grandson. Most of her married life was passed elsewhere, and Annesley fell into the neglected condition which Irving describes. Mary's husband, the maligned Musters, instead of hating the place and seeking to destroy its identity, preferred it to his other property, and spent many years after his wife's death in restoring and beautifying it, taking pains to preserve the grounds and the main portion of the mansion in the condition in which his wife had known them in her maidenhood. This became the beloved home of his later years, and here he died. This mansion of the " Dream" stands upon an elevation overlooking many acres of picturesque park. It is a great, rambling pile of motley architecture, obviously erected by different generations of Chaworths to suit their varying needs and tastes, but the walls are overgrown with clambering vines, which conceal the touch of time and impart to the structure an aspect of harmonious beauty. The principal façade which presents along the court is imposing and stately, but on every side are pointed gables, stone balustrades, and picturesque walls. The interior arrangement of the body of the house remains precisely as Mary knew it, even the decorations of some of the rooms having been preserved by the considerate love of her husband and descendants; and here, despite the averment of a Byron-biographer that " every relic of her ancient family was sold and scattered to the winds," the Chaworth plate, portraits, and other belongings are religiously cherished. We were first invited to the place to see these while they were yet displayed by the maid in whose arms Mary died. Upon the walls of the great lower hall are many family pictures, among them that of the Chaworth whom Byron's great-uncle had slain. It was this portrait that Byron feared would come out of its frame to haunt him if he remained here over-night. From the hall low stairs lead to the apartments. At the right is Mary's sitting-room, where Byron spent many hours beside her, listening entranced while she played to him upon the piano which stood in the farther corner. It is a pleasant apartment, its windows looking out upon the garden-beds Mary tended, which we see now ablaze with the flowers known to have been her favorites. In this room, which " her smiles had made a heaven to him," Byron, years afterward, saw Mary for the last time and kissed for its mother's sake " the child that ought to have been his."

A Literary Pilgrimage

On this occasion she made the inquiry which prompted the lines, "To Mrs. Musters, on being asked my reason for quitting England in the spring." This last painful interview is recalled in the poems "Well, Thou art Happy" and "I've seen my Bride Another's Bride." Above the hall is the large drawing-room, where we see several portraits of Mary, which represent her as a most beautiful woman, with a pathetically sweet and winning face,—by no means the "wicked-looking cat" which Byron's jealous wife described. Here, too, are pictures of her husband which fully justify his popular sobriquet, "handsome Jack Musters." Physically they were an admirably matched pair. Out of the drawing-room is the "antique oratory" of the poem, a small apartment above the entrance-porch, pictured as the scene of Byron's parting with Mary after her announcement of her betrothal. Byron was cordially welcomed at Annesley; the family were his relatives, and all of them, save that young lady herself, would gladly have had him marry the heiress. Among the guest-chambers is one, called of yore the blue room, which during one summer—after his fear of the family portraits had been subdued by the greater fear of meeting "bogles" on his homeward way—Byron often occupied. Here he incensed Nanny the housekeeper by allowing his dog to sleep upon the bed and soil her neat counterpanes. Another servant, "old Joe," tired of sitting up at night to wait upon him, finally frightened him away by means of some hideous nocturnal noises, which he assured the young poet proceeded from "spooks out of the kirk-yard," —Byron's superstition doubtless suggesting the ruse.

Giant trees overtop the chimneys and bower the walls of the venerable mansion. The garden which Irving found matted and wild was long ago restored by Musters to its former beauty of turf, foliage, and flower. A grand terrace,—one of the finest in England,—with brick walls and carved balustrades of stone mantled and draped with ivy, lies at the right, with broad steps leading down to the garden where Byron delighted to linger with Mary during the swift hours of one too brief summer. Beneath the terrace is a door, carefully protected by Musters and his descendants, which Byron daily used as a target and in which we see the marks of bullets from his pistol. The grounds are extensive and beautifully diversified by copses of great trees and grassy glades where deer feed amid myriad witcheries of leaf and bloom. Half a mile from the Hall is a shrine that will attract the sentimental prowler, Byron's diadem hill. Projecting from the extremity of a long line of eminences, it is a landmark to the countryside and overlooks the living landscape which the poet depicted in lines throbbing with life and beauty. From its acclivity we see much of his ancestral Newstead, the adjoining fair acres of Annesley which he would have added to his own, the tower and chimneys of the Hall rising among clustering oaks : beyond these darkly wooded hills decline to the valley, along which we look—past parks, villages, and the church where Byron sleeps—to the spires of the city. As we contemplate the vista from the spot where stood the two bright " beings in the hues of youth," we have about us a ring of dark firs, the " diadem of trees in circular array" pictured in the " Dream," apparently unchanged since the day the maiden and the youth here met for the last time before her marriage. The Byron-writers have united in denouncing Musters for denuding this hill-top in a splenetic endeavor to prevent its identification as the scene of the interview described in the poem. In truth, we owe the preservation of the features which identify this romantic spot to the very hand which the author of " Crayon Miscellany" avers is " execrated by every poetic pilgrim." When natural causes were rapidly destroying the grove, Musters caused its removal and replaced it by saplings grown from cones of the old trees, each fir of the present beautiful diadem being sedulously rooted upon the site of its lineal ancestor. Musters had much greater reason to regard this spot with romantic tenderness than had the poet; here he enjoyed many stolen interviews with his sweetheart, for he was forbidden to see her in her home, and she, perverse and persistent in her passion for him, came here daily with the hope of meeting him and watched for his approach along the valley. Upon the very occasion the poem describes, she waited here, " Looking afar if yet her lover's steed kept pace with her expectancy," and merely tolerated the company of the "gaby" boy Byron until Musters might arrive. The latter had no reason for the irritable jealousy toward Byron which has been attributed to him, and there is no evidence that he evinced or entertained such a feeling. He freely invited the poet to his house, rode and swam with him, preserved the few Byron mementos at Annesley, and protected the tombs of Byron's ancestors at Colwick. So much of untruth has been published anent the Byron-Chaworth-Musters matter, and especially concerning the attitude of the lady toward Byron and the conditions of her subsequent life, that it is pleasant, even at this late day, to be able to record upon un-

doubted evidence that her loving admiration for
her husband ceased only with her life.

On the bank of the silvery Trent, three
miles from Nottingham, is Colwick Hall, where
Mary's married life was spent. This was an
ancient seat of the Byrons, said to have been
lost by them at the card-table. Mary's home
was an imposing mansion, with lofty cupola,
balustraded roofs, and stately pediments upheld
by Ionic columns. From the front windows
we look across a wide expanse of sun-kissed
meadow beyond the river, while at the back
rocky cliffs rise steeply and are tufted by overhanging woods. The Hall was attacked and
pillaged in 1831 by a Luddite mob, from whom
poor Mary escaped half naked into the shrubbery and lay concealed in the cold wet night.
The exposure and terror of this event impaired
her reason, and caused her death the next year
at Wiverton, another seat of the Chaworths,
where her descendants reside. Close by the
mansion at Colwick, now a summer resort, was
the old gray church, with battlemented tower,
where Mary was married, and where she lies in
death with her husband and his kindred, near
the burial-vault of the ancestors of the lame
boy who linked her name to deathless verse.
At the side of the altar a beautiful monumental
tablet, bearing a graceful female figure and a

laudatory inscription, is placed in memory of the " star of Annesley," whose brightness went out in distraction and gloom.

To Byron's early passion and its failure we owe some of the sweetest and tenderest of his songs ; and it has been believed that the memory of that defeat adapted his thoughts to their highest flights and gave added pathos and beauty to his noblest work. Thus all the world were gainers by his disappointment, and evidence is lacking that either the lady or the lover was a loser.

THE HOME OF CHILDE HAROLD

*Newstead—Byron's Apartments—Relics and Reminders—Ghosts—
Ruins — The Young Oak — Dog's Tomb — Devil's Wood—
Irving—Livingstone—Stanley—Joaquin Miller.*

HOWEVER alluring other haunts of Byron
may be found, the " hall of his fathers"
must remain paramount in the interest and affection of his admirers. The stanzas he addressed
to that venerable pile, the graphic description
in " Don Juan," the plaintive allusions in " Childe
Harold," its own romantic history as a mediæval
fortress and shrine, and its association with the
bard who inherited its lands and dwelt beneath
its battlements, render Newstead Abbey a Mecca
to which the steps of pilgrims tend. It came
to the Byrons by royal gift, and in the middle of
the last century was inherited by the poet's predecessor the Wicked Byron, who killed his
neighbor of Annesley and so desolated the Abbey
that the only spot sheltered from the storms was
a corner of the scullery where he breathed out
his wretched life. The poet occupied the place
at intervals for twenty years, and then sold it to
Colonel Wildman, who had been his form-fellow
at Harrow, and to whom we are mainly indebted
for the restoration of the edifice and the preserva-

NEWSTEAD ABBEY

THE HOME OF CHILDE HAROLD

HOWEVER alluring other haunts of Byron may be found, the " hall of his fathers" must remain paramount in the interest and affec-
t r of his admirers. The stanzas he addressed
·· ... able ... graphic description
.. .. " Childe
... .rdi. al
.. .. wicl the
... .. 'e. .th
.. .. . M cca
t ·· .. . It ame
to the k ror .. dd· o
the (a t cent ir l y .. .:t's predecessor the M G. r r, who killed his
neighbor of Ann.. ... so desolated the Abbey
that the only spot .h.h.red from the storms was
a corner of the scullery where he breathed out
his wretched life. The poet occupied the plac:
at intervals for twenty years, and then sold it 'o
Colonel Wildman, who had been his form ..lo v
at Harrow, and to whom we are mainly : ..bt d
for the restoration of the edifice and the ..crva-

tion of every memento of the poet and his race. At the death of Wildman the Abbey became the property of Colonel W. F. Webb, a sharer in Livingstone's explorations, who gathers here a brilliant circle of authors, artists, travellers, and wits whose gayety dispels the hoary and ghostly associations of the place.

From the boundary of the estate a broad avenue, lined with noble trees, leads to an inner park of eight hundred acres, among whose sylvan beauties our way lies, through verdant glades and under leafy boughs whose shadows the sunshine prints upon the path, until we see, from the verge of the wood, the noble pile rising amid an environment of lawn and lake, grove and garden. It is a vast stone structure, composed of motley parts joined " by no quite lawful marriage of the arts" into an harmonious and impressive whole. The western façade is the one usually pictured, because it contains the Byron apartments and best displays the characteristic features of the edifice, having a castellated tower at one extremity, while to the other is joined the ruined chapel front which, as an example of its style, is rivalled in architectural value only by St. Mary's at York. This Newstead fragment, retaining its perfect proportions, its noble windows, its gray statue of the Virgin and " God-born Child" in the high niche of the gable,—the whole

draped and garlanded with ivy which conceals
the scars of Cromwell's cannon-balls,—is a vision
of unique beauty.   From the Gothic door-way
of the mansion we are admitted to a gallery
with a low-vaulted roof of stone upheld by
massive columns.   This was the crypt of the
abbot's dormitory ; it adjoins the cloisters, and,
like them, was used by the Wicked Byron as a
stable for cattle.   It is now adorned with the
spoils of African deserts, trophies of the mighty
huntsman who now inhabits the Abbey.   One
of these, the skin of a noble lion, is said to
have belonged to a beast which had mutilated
Livingstone and was standing above his body
when a ball from Webb's rifle laid him low and
saved the great explorer.   From the crypt, stone
stairs lead to the corridors above the cloisters :
in Byron's time entrance was between a bear
and a wolf chained on these stairs and menacing
the guest from either side.   Out of the corridor
adjoining the chapel ruin a spiral stairway ascends
to a plain and sombre suite of rooms, once the
abbot's lodgings, but cherished now because
they were the private apartments of Byron.
His chamber is neither large nor elegant, its walls
are plainly papered, and its single oriel window
is shaded by a faded curtain.   The room remains
as Byron last occupied it : his carpet is upon the
floor ; the carved bedstead, with its gilt posts

and lordly coronets, is the one brought by him from college; its curtains and coverings are those he used; above the mantel is the mirror which often reflected his handsome features. We sit in his embroidered arm-chair by the window, overlooking lawn and lake and the wood he planted, and write out upon his plain table the memoranda from which this article is prepared. The tourist is told that the chamber has never been used since Byron left it; but Irving occupied it for some time, as his letters to his brother declare, and a few years ago our Joaquin Miller lay here in Byron's bed, and saw, in the moonbeams sharply reflected from the mirror into his face, an explanation of the ghostly apparitions which Byron beheld in this glass. In the adjoining room are a portrait of the poet's " corporeal pastor," Jackson, in arena costume, and a painting of Byron's valet, Joe Murray, a bright-looking fellow of pleasing face and faultless attire. This room was sometime occupied by Byron's pretty page, whom the housekeeper believed to be a girl in masquerade: this page was introduced elsewhere as the poet's younger brother Gordon, and an attempt has been made to identify her with the mysterious " Thyrza" of his poems, and with " Astarte" also. The third room of the suite, Byron's dressing-room and study, was one of the haunts

of the goblin friar who was heard stalking amid
the dim cloisters or in the apartments above.
Byron's room here is the Gothic chamber of
the Norman abbey where " Don Juan" slept
and dreamed of Aurora Raby, and the corridor
is the "gallery of sombre hue" where he pur-
sued the sable phantom and captured a very
material duchess. Directly beneath is a panelled apartment of moderate dimensions which
was Byron's dining-room and the scene of many
a revel when the monk's skull, brimming with
wine, was sent round by the poet's guests. His
sideboard is still here, his heavy table remains
in the middle of the room, and the famous skull,
mounted as a drinking-cup and inscribed with
the familiar anacreontic, is carefully preserved.
The library is a stately and spacious apartment :
here, among many mementos of the poet, Ada
Byron first heard a poem of her father's ; here
Byron's Italian friend la Guiccioli made notes
for her " Recollections," and here Livingstone
penned portions of the books which record his
explorations. In the grand hall we see the
elevated chimney-piece beneath which Byron
and his guests heaped so great a fire, on the first
night of his occupancy of the Abbey, that its
destruction was threatened. This superb apartment, the old dormitory of the monks, was
used by the poet as a shooting-gallery, and was

one of the haunts of his "Black Friar." The drawing-room of the mansion is palatial in dimensions and furnishing. Its panels and grotesque carvings have been restored, and this ancient room, once the refectory of the monks and later the hay-loft of the Wicked Byron, is now a marvel of elegance. Here is the familiar portrait of Byron at twenty-three, an earlier watercolor picturing him in college gown, and a later bust in marble. Here by her desire the body of Ada Byron lay in state, and from here it was borne to rest beside her father at near-by Hucknall, more than realizing the closing stanzas of the third canto of "Childe Harold."

In these stately rooms and in the adjoining corridors are numerous priceless relics of the immortal bard; among them, the cap, belt, and cimeter he wore in Greece; his foils, spurs, stirrups, and boxing-gloves; a painting of his famous dog Boatswain; the bronze candlesticks from his writing-table and the table upon which were written "Bards and Reviewers," poems of "Hours of Idleness," "Hebrew Melodies," and portions of his masterpiece, "Childe Harold." Preserved here, with Byron's will, unpublished letters, and scraps of verse, are papers which indicate that the poet's *chef-d'œuvre* was originally designed for private circulation and was entitled "Childe Byron." An interesting relic is a section of the noted "twin-tree" bearing the names "Byron—Augusta" carved by the poet at his last visit to the Abbey. Our own Barnum once visited the place and offered Wildman five hundred pounds for this double tree (then standing in the grove), intending to remove it for exhibition; the colonel indignantly replied that five thousand would not purchase it, and that "the man capable of such a project deserved to be gibbeted." Here, too, are the portrait of the first lord of Newstead, "John Byron-the-Little-with-the-Great-Beard;" the huge iron knocker in use on the door of the Abbey seven centuries ago; a collection of mediæval armor and weapons; some personal belongings of Livingstone, and many specimens of fauna and flora gathered by him and Webb in the dark continent. One vaulted apartment of exquisite proportions, erst the sanctuary of the abbot, and later Byron's dog-kennel, is now the chapel of the household. Newstead has been the abode of royalty, and holds rooms in which, from the time of Edward III., kings have often lodged. We see the chamber occupied by Ada Byron during her visit; another, adorned with quaint carvings and once haunted by Byron-of-the-Great-Beard, was used by Irving. The noble chambers contain richly carved furniture, costly tapestries, and beds of such altitude that

steps are provided for scaling them. The hangings of one bed belonged to Prince Rupert, and
its counterpane was embroidered by Mary Queen
of Scots.

In the centre of the edifice is the quadrangular
court, surrounded by a series of low-vaulted
arcades, once the stables of the Wicked Byron
and long ago the " cloisters dim and damp" of
the monks whose dust moulders now beneath
the pavement. One crypt-like cell which holds
the boilers for heating the mansion was Byron's
swimming-bath. In the middle of the court
the ancient stone fountain, with its grotesque
sculptures of saints and monsters, graven by the
patient toil of the monks, still sends out sprays
of coolness.

We spend delightful hours loitering in the
ancient gardens of the friars and about their
ruined chapel. Through its mighty window,
" yawning all desolate," pours a flood of western
light upon the turf that covers the holy ground
where congregations knelt in worship ; while,
amid the dust of the priests and near the
site of the altar where they " raised their pious
voices but to pray," Byron's dog lies in a tomb
far handsomer than that which holds his noble
master. It was in excavating Boatswain's grave
that Byron found the skull afterward used as a
drinking-cup. The dog's monument consists of

a wide pedestal, surmounted by a panelled altar-stone which upholds a funeral urn and bears Byron's familiar eulogistic inscription and the misanthropic stanzas ending with the lines,—

"To mark a friend's remains these stones arise;
  I never knew but one, and here he lies."

Other panels were designed to bear the epitaph of Byron, who directed in his will (1811) that he should be buried in this spot with his valet and dog; it is said to have been discovered that the poet had made careful preparation for his entombment here, the stone trestles and slab to support his coffin being in place upon the pavement, but the sale of Newstead led to his interment elsewhere, and faithful Murray—who declined to lie here "alone with the dog"—sleeps near his master.

The gardens of the Abbey lie about its ancient walls: here are the fish-pools of the monks; the noble terrace; the "Young Oak" of Byron's poem, planted by his hands and now grown into a large and graceful tree; other trees rooted by Livingstone and Stanley while guests here. At one side is a grove of beeches and yews, in whose gloomy recesses the Wicked Byron erected leaden statues of Pan and Pandora, of which the rustics were so afraid that they would not go near them after nightfall, and which are still respectfully spoken of in the servants' hall as " Mr. and Mrs. Devil." Before the mansion lies the lucid lake described in " Don Juan:" the forest that shades its shore and sweeps over the farther hill-side was planted by Byron to repair the spoliation of his uncle, and is called the " Poet's Wood." Upon some of the farms of the domain live descendants of Nancy Smith, whom Irving's readers will remember, her son having married despite his mother's protest and reared a family. One aged servitor claims to remember Irving's visit, and opines " the old colonel [Wildman] thought him a very fine man—for an American." He recounts some peccadilloes of Joe Murray, traditional among the servants, which show that worthy to have been less precise in morals than in dress. The ancient Byron estates were among the haunts of one whose exploits inspired a book of ballads, and we here see Robin Hood's cave and other reminders of the bold outlaw and his " merrie men in Lyncolne greene."

Such, briefly, is the condition of Byron's ancestral home as it appears nearly eighty years after he saw it for the last time. Besides the charms which won his affection and made him relinquish the Abbey with such poignant regret, it holds for us an added spell in that it has been the habitation of a transcendent genius. Where

A Literary Pilgrimage

Wildman's fortune failed his wishes the present owner has supplemented his work, until the vast pile now gleams with more than its ancient splendor ; and, as we take a last view through a glade whose beauty fitly frames the picture of the restored mansion, we trust that somehow and somewhere Byron knows that his hope for his beloved Newstead is accomplished :

> " Haply thy sun emerging yet may shine,
>   Thee to irradiate with meridian ray ;
> Hours splendid as the past may still be thine,
>   And bless thy future as thy former day."

WARWICKSHIRE: THE LOAM-
SHIRE OF GEORGE ELIOT

Miss Mulock – Butler – Somervile – Dyer – Rugby – Homes of George Eliot – Scenes of Tales – Cheverel – Shepperton – Milly's Grave–Paddiford–Milby–Coventry, etc.–Characters–Incidents.

SOME one has said that to write about Warwickshire is to write about Shakespeare.
True, the transcending fame of the bard of Avon
gives the places associated with his life and genius
pre-eminence, but the literary rambler will find
in this heart of England other shrines worthy
of homage. Inevitably our pilgrimage includes
the Stratford scenes,—from the birthplace and
the Hathaway cottage to the fane where all the
world bows at Shakespeare's tomb,—but, resolutely repressing the inclination to describe again
these oft-described resorts, we fare to less familiar shrines : to the birthplace of the author of
" Hudibras" and the haunts and tomb of Somervile, poet of " The Chase" and " Rural Sports ;"
to the Rhynhill of Braddon's tale and the Kenil-
worth of Scott's matchless romance ; to Bilton,
where Addison sometime dwelt, and the Cal-
thorpe home of Dyer, bard of " Grongar Hill"
and " The Fleece," where we find his garden
and a tree he planted which shades now his battle-

mented old church; to Rugby, where we see the dormitory of "Tom Brown" Hughes, the class-rooms he shared with Clough, Matthew Arnold, and Dean Stanley, the grave of the beloved Dr. Arnold in the "Rugby Chapel" of his son's poem.

At Avonmouth we find the Norton Bury of "John Halifax," and the old inn where Dinah Mulock lived while writing this her popular tale. The inn garden holds the yew hedge of the novel, "fifteen feet high and as many thick," and the sward over which crept the lame Phineas: sitting there, we see the view the boy admired,—the old Abbey tower, the mill of Abel Fletcher, the river where the famished rioters fought for the grains the grim old man had flung into the water, the green level of the Ham dotted with cattle, the white sails of the encircling Severn, the farther sweep of country extending to the distant hills,—and hear the sweet-toned Abbey chimes and the lazy whir of the mill which sounded so pleasantly in Phineas's ears.

"John Halifax" was published simultaneously with another tale of Warwickshire life, "Amos Barton." We are newly come from the London homes of George Eliot and her grave on the Highgate hill-side, and now, as we traverse sweet Avonvale, we gladly remember that Shakespeare's shire is hers as well. A jaunt of a score of miles from Stratford brings us to the scenes amid which she was born and grew to physical and mental maturity. Our course by "Avon's stream," bowered by willows or bordered by meads, lies past the noble park where Shakespeare did not steal deer and the palace of his Justice Shallow where he was not arraigned for poaching. (We find it as impossible to keep Shakespeare out of our MS. as did Mr. Dick of "Copperfield" to keep Charles I. out of the memorial.) Beyond Charlecote is storied Warwick Castle, with the old mansion of Compton Wyniates, dwelling of the royalist knight of Scott's "Woodstock," not far away. Beyond these again we come to the Coventry region and the frontier of the "Loamshire" whose characteristics are imaged and whose traditions, phases of life, and scenery are wrought with tender touch into poem and tale by George Eliot and so made familiar to all the world. Warwickshire scenery is not sublime; Dr. Arnold characterized it as "an endless monotony of enclosed fields and hedgerow trees." While its landscapes lack striking features, theirs is the quiet, unobtrusive beauty which Hawthorne loved and which for us is full of restful charm. Across sunny vales and gentle eminences we look away to the far-off Malvern Hills, whose shadowy outlines bound many a "Loamshire" landscape. We see vistas of low-lying meads with circling "lines of willows marking the watercourses;" of slumberous expanses of green or golden fields; of villages grouped about gray church-towers; of groves of venerable woods,—survivors of Shakespeare's "Forest of Arden" which erst clothed the countryside. We find it, indeed, "worth the journey hither only to see the hedgerows,"— green, fragrant walls of hawthorn which border lane and highway, bound garden and field. With their gleaming boughs rayed by bright blossoms and festooned with interlacing vines, these barriers are often marvels of beauty and strength. Between miles of such hedgerows, and beneath lines of overshading elms, a highway running northward from the town of Godiva and "Peeping Tom" brings us to the great Arbury property of the Newdigates, where we find the South Farm homestead in which Robert Evans—newly appointed agent of the estate— temporarily placed his family, and where, in the room at the left of the central chimney-stack, at five o'clock on the morning of St. Cecilia's day, 1819, his youngest child, Mary Ann, was born. It is a broad-eaved, many-gabled, two-storied structure of stuccoed stone, with trim hedges and flower-bordered garden-beds about it, a wider environment of lawn and woodland, and colonnades of the elms which figure in her poems

and were already venerable when she saw the
light beneath their shade. On the same estate,
near the highway between Bedworth and Nuneaton, is Griff House, "the warm nest where
her affections were fledged," to which she was
removed at the age of four months, and where
her first score years of life were passed. It is a
pleasant and picturesque double-storied mansion
of brick, quaint and comfortable. Massy ivy
mantles its walls, climbs to its gables, overruns
its roofs, peeps in at its tiny-paned casements;
doves coo upon its ridges. About it flowers
shine from their setting in the emerald of the
lawn, and great trees open their leaves to the sunshine and winds of summer. Spacious rooms lie
upon either side of the entrance: of the one at
the left, the novelist gives us a glimpse in "The
Mill on the Floss." It is a home-like apartment,
with low walls and a pleasant fireplace; it was the
dining-room and sitting-room also in the days
when "the little wench" Mary Ann was the pet
of the household. Here she acted charades
with her brother Isaac and astonished the family
by repeating stories from "Miller's Jest Book,"
a treasured volume of hers in that early time.
We learn from Maggie Tulliver—in whose
childhood is pictured the author's inner life as a
child—that Defoe's "History of the Devil"
was another of Mary Ann's juvenile favorites,

and her relatives preserve the worn copy she used to read here before this fireplace with her father, containing the pictures of the drowning witch and the devil which little Maggie explained to Mr. Riley in "The Mill on the Floss." Here, years afterward, Mary Ann heard, from her "Methodist Aunt Samuel," the thrilling story of the girl executed for child-murder, which was the germ of the great romance "Adam Bede." The aunt, who had been a preacher in earlier life, remained at Griff for some time, and George Eliot has told us that the character of Dinah Morris grew out of her recollections of this relative. It may be noted that in real life Dinah married Seth Bede, Adam being drawn in part—like Caleb Garth—from the novelist's father. In this same room, but a few years ago, the "Brother" of the poem, who played here at charades with little Mary Ann, suddenly ex-pired in his chair but a few minutes after his return from "Shepperton Church." The win-dows of Mary Ann's chamber command a reach of the coach-road of "Felix Holt" and a farther vista of woodlands and fields; in another chamber is the mahogany bed beneath which she was once found hidden to avoid going to school. In the roof is the attic which was Maggie Tulliver's retreat, where she kept her wooden doll with the nails in its head, and here is the chimney-stack against which that vicarious sufferer was ground and beaten. The death of her mother, Mrs. Hackit of "Barton," made Mary Ann mistress of Griff at sixteen. At Griff's gates stood the cottage of Dame Moore's school, where the novelist began her education, and where years after she used to collect the children of the vicinage for religious instruction each Sabbath. A son of Mrs. Moore lately lived not far away, and had more to say in praise of "Mary Hann" than of her surviving kinsfolk, who seem ashamed of their relationship to the novelist. In a shaded part of the garden lately stood a bower with a stone table, which George Eliot doubtless had in mind when she described the finding of Casaubon's corpse in the arbor at Lowick. The exhausted quarries in the shale close by, a resort of Mary Ann's girlhood, are the "Red Deeps" where Maggie met her lover; the "brown canal" of the poem winds through the near hollow; and beyond it, on "an apology for an elevation of ground," is the "College" workhouse to which Amos Barton walked through the sleet to read prayers. Not far distant is Arbury Hall, seat of the Newdigates, for whom the tenant of Griff was and is agent. This is the Cheverel Manor of "Gilfil," an imposing castellated structure of gray stone, with flanking towers and great mullioned windows of multishaped panes, famous for its elaborately decorated ceilings. That George Eliot had often been within this mansion is shown by her familiarity with the arrangement and ornamentation of the rooms, accurately described as scenes of many incidents of the tale. In the grounds, too, the imagery of the " Love Story" may be perfectly realized : here are the lawn where little Caterina sat with Lady Cheverel, and the shimmering pool, with its swans and water-lilies, which was searched for her corpse the morning of her flight ; at a little distance we find " Mosslands," and the cottage of the gardener to which the dead body of Wybrow was carried ; and, farther away, the spot under giant limes where the poor girl, coming to meet her recreant lover "with a dagger in her dress and murder in her heart," found him lying dead in the path, his hand clutching the dark leaves, his eyes unheeding the " sunlight that darted upon them between the boughs." A touching incident in the life of a former owner of Arbury was made the plot of Otway's tragedy " The Orphan."

A mile northward from Griff is the quaint church of Chilvers Coton, where Mary Ann was christened at the age of a week, where a little later her " devotional patience" was fostered by smuggled bread-and-butter, and where as child and woman she worshipped for twenty years. It is a massive stone edifice with Gothic windows, one of them being a memorial of the wife of Isaac Evans, and with a square tower rising above its low roofs ; at one corner, "a flight of stone steps, with their wooden rail running up the outer wall," still leads to the children's gallery as in the days of Gilfil and Amos Barton, for this is the Shepperton Church of the tales. Within we see the memorials of Rev. Gilpin Ebdell (thought to be Gilfil) and of the original of Mrs. Farquhar ; the place where Gilfil read his sermons from manuscript "rather yellow and worn at the edges," and where Barton later "preached without book." About the renovated fane is the church-yard, with its grassy mounds and mouldering tombstones, one of which, protected by a paling and shaded by leafy boughs, is crowned by a funeral urn and marks the spot where Milly was laid,—"the sweet mother with her baby in her arms,"—the grave to which Barton came back an old man with Patty supporting his infirm steps. Its inscription is to "Emma, beloved wife of Revd. John Gwyther, B.A.," curate here in George Eliot's girlhood : during his incumbency the community felt aggrieved for his wife on account of the prolonged stay at the parsonage of a strange woman who, years after, was described as Countess Czerlaski by one who as a child had seen her here. Not far from Milly's monument the parents of George Eliot lie in one grave, with Isaac, the "Brother" of her poem, sleeping near. By the church-yard wall stands the pleasant ivy-grown parsonage to which Gilfil brought his dark-eyed bride, and where, after brief months of happiness, he lived the long years of solitude and sorrow. We see the cosy parlor—smelling no longer of his or Barton's pipe—where the lonely old man sat with his dog, and above, its pretty window overlooking the garden, the chamber where he tenderly cherished the dainty belongings of his dead wife with the unused baby-clothes her fingers had fashioned, and where, in another tale, is laid one of the most affecting and high-wrought scenes in all fiction, the death of Milly Barton.

A half-mile distant lies the village of Attleboro, where, at the age of five, Mary Ann was sent to Miss Lathorn's school; and a mile southward from Griff, in a region blackened by pits, is the town of Bedworth,—"dingy with coal-dust and noisy with looms,"—whose men "walk with knees bent outward from squatting in the mine," and whose haggard, overworked women and dirty children and cottages are pathetically pictured in "Felix Holt." Obviously the changes of the half-century which has elapsed since George Eliot knew its wretchedness have wrought little improvement in this place, over which her nephew is rector: we see pale, hungry faces in the streets, squalor in the poor dwellings, proofs of pinching poverty everywhere. A little beyond Chilvers Coton we find the market-town of Nuneaton, the Milby of the romances. The shaking of hand-looms is less noticeable now than in George Eliot's school-days here, factories having supplanted the cottage industry; but the dingy, smoky town, with its environment of flat fields, is still "nothing but dreary prose." Here we find, near the church, "The Elms" of her girlhood, a tall brick edifice embowered with ivy; on its garden side, the long low-ceiled school-room, with its heavy beams, broad windows, and plain furniture, where she was four years a pupil; the dormitory whence she beheld the riot which she describes in the election-riot at Treby in "Felix Holt." Another vision of her girlhood here was a "tall, black-coated young clergyman-in-embryo," Liggins by name, who afterward claimed the authorship of her books and so far imposed upon the public that a subscription was made for him. Mrs. Gaskell was one of the last to relinquish the belief that Liggins was George Eliot. He spent most of his time drinking, but did his own house-work, and was found by a deputation of literary admirers washing his slop-basin at the pump. All about us at Nuneaton lie familiar objects: the cosy Bull Inn is the " Red Lion" where, in the opening of "Janet's Repentance," Dempser is discovered in theologic discussion, and from whose window he harangued the anti-Tyranite mob; the fine old church, with its beautiful oaken carvings, is the sanctuary where Mr. Crewe, in brown Brutus wig, delivered his " inaudible sermons," and where Mr. Elty preached later; adjoining is the parsonage, erst redolent of Crewe's tobacco, where Janet helped his deaf wife to spread the luncheon for the bishop, and where, in the time of Elty, Barton came to the sessions of the " Clerical Meeting and Book Society;" on this Church street, "Orchard Street" of Eliot, a quaint stuccoed house with casement windows was Dempser's home, whence he thrust his wife at midnight into the darkness and cold; the arched passage near by is that through which she fled to the haven of Mrs. Pettifer's house. A little way westward amid the pits is Stockingford, " Paddiford" of the tale, and the chapel where Mr. Tyran preached. A cousin of George Eliot's was recently a coal-master in this vicinity.

Eight miles from Griff is Coventry, where our companion is one who had met Rossetti there forty years before. George Eliot was sometime a pupil of Miss Franklin's school, lately standing in Little Park Street, and saw there that lady's father, whom she described as Rev. Rufus Lyon of Treby Chapel. His diminutive legs, large head, and other peculiarities are yet remembered by some who were in the school; his home is accurately pictured in "Felix Holt." In the Foleshill suburb we find the stone villa of Birds Grove, which was the home of the novelist after Isaac Evans had succeeded his father at Griff. The house has been enlarged, but the apartments she knew are little changed: a plain little room above the entrance, whose window looked beyond the tree-tops to the superb spire of St. Michael's Church,—where Kemble and Siddons were married,—was her study, in which, despite her tasks as her father's housewife and nurse, she accomplished much literary work. At the right of the window stood her desk, with an ivory crucifix above it, and here her translation of Strauss's "Leben Jesu," undertaken through the persuasion of her friends at Rosehill, was written. Some portions of this work she found distressing; she declared to Mrs. Bray that nothing but the sight of the Christ image enabled her to endure dissecting the beautiful story of the crucifixion. Adjoining the study is her modest bedchamber, and beyond it that of her father, where during many months of sickness she was his sole attendant, often sitting the long night through at his bedside with her hand in his. The grounds are little changed, save that the occupant has removed much of the foliage which formerly shrouded the mansion, but some of George Eliot's favorite trees remain on the lawn. Half a mile away is the pretty villa of Rosehill, whilom the home of Mrs. Bray and her sister Sara Hennel, who were the most valued friends of the novelist's young-womanhood and exerted the strongest influence upon her life. Her letters to these friends constitute a great part of Cross's " Life." At Rosehill she met Chapman, Mackay, Robert Owen, Combe, Thackeray, Herbert Spencer, and others of like genius, and here she spent a day with Emerson and wrote next day, " I have seen Emerson—the first *man* I have ever seen." Sara Hennel testifies that Emerson was impressed with Miss Evans and declared, " That young lady has a serious soul." When he asked her, " What one book do you like best ?" and she replied, " Rousseau's Confessions," he quickly responded, " So do I : there is a point of sympathy between us." After her father's death she was for sixteen months a resident at Rosehill, and there wrote, among other things, the review of Mackay's " Progress of the Intellect." Financial reverses caused the Brays long ago to relinquish this beautiful home, but some of this household were lately living in another suburb of Coventry and receiving an annuity bequeathed by George Eliot. Here, too, lately resided another old-time friend, the Mary Sibtree of the novelist's Coventry days, to whom were addressed some of the letters used by Cross.

In 1851 George Eliot left this circle of friends to become an inmate of Chapman's house in London, returning to them for occasional visits for the next few years; then came her union with Lewes, after which the loved scenes of her youth knew her no more in the flesh; but the allusions to them which run like threads of gold through all her work show how oft she revisited them in " shadowy spirit form."

YORKSHIRE SHRINES: DO-THEBOYS HALL AND ROKEBY

Village of Bowes—Dickens—Squeers's School—The Master and his Family—Haunt of Scott.

FROM the familiar shrines of Cumberland, the lakeside haunts of Wordsworth, Southey, and Coleridge, a journey across a wild moorland region—from whose higher crags we see through the fog-rifts the German Ocean and the Irish Sea—brings us into Gretavale, on the northern border of great Yorkshire. In the upper portion of the valley, among the outlying spurs of the Pennines, the storied Greta flows at the foot of a bleak, treeless hill on whose summit we find the village of Bowes. This was the Lavatræ of the Romans, who for three centuries had here a station, and remains of great Roman works may still be traced in the vicinage; but to the literary pilgrim Bowes is chiefly of interest as representing " the delightful village of Dotheboys" described in Squeers's advertisement of his school in " Nicholas Nickleby." The aspect of the village is dreary and desolate in the extreme. A single street, steep and straight, bordered by straggling houses of dull gray stone, extends along the hill, which is crowned by the church and an ancient castle : the dun moors decline steeply on every side, leaving the treeless village dismal and bare and often exposed to a wind " fit to knock a man off his legs," as Squeers said to Nicholas. In the midst of the village stands a cosy inn, where Dickens for some time lodged and was visited by John Browdie, and where we are shown the wainscoted apartment in which some portion of " Nickleby" was noted. At the time of Dickens's sojourn here, Bowes was the centre of the pernicious cheap-school system which he came to expose, and half the houses of the village were "academies" similar to that of Squeers : among them one is pointed out as being the place where Cobden was a pupil. But most interesting of all is the large house at the top of the hill which Dickens depicted as Dotheboys Hall,—by which name it was long known among the older dwellers of the place,— a long, heavy, two-storied, dingy structure of stone, with many windows along its front, and presenting, despite its bowering vines and trees, an aspect so chill and cheerless that one can scarcely conceive of a more depressing domicile for the neglected children who once thronged it. Through an archway at one end could be seen the pump which was frozen on the first morning of Nicholas's stay, and beyond it the garden

which, by a surprising mistake, Dickens represents a pupil to be weeding on a freezing winter's
day.

A few residents of the neighborhood remember the "measther" of Dotheboys Hall; his
name, like Squeers's, was of one syllable and
began with S; in person he was not like Squeers,
nor was he an ignorant man. A quondam pupil
of the school informed the writer that Johnny
S. was fairly drawn as Wackford Squeers, but
Miss S. was a young lady of considerable refine-
ment and was in no sense like the spiteful Fanny
of the tale. Squeers had the largest of the
schools, and, besides rooms in the adjoining
house, he hired barns in which to lodge his
many pupils. A farm attached to his house
was cultivated by the scholars, whose food was
chiefly oatmeal: scanty diet and liberal flogging
was the portion of all who displeased the master.
According to local belief, this school was not so
bad as some of its neighbors, and no one of the
schools realized all the wretchedness which
Dickens portrays; yet, despite the author's
avowal that Squeers was a representative of a
class, and not an individual, the popular identification of this school as the typical Dotheboys,
and the odium consequent thereupon, wrought
its speedy ruin and the death of the master and
mistress. The latter result is to be deplored, for

the reason that in the case of this pair the abhorrence seems to have been not wholly deserved. Two charges, at least, which affected them most painfully—that of goading the boys to suicide and that of feeding them upon the flesh of diseased cattle—were, by the testimony of their neighbors, unfounded so far as the proprietors of this school were concerned. Relatives of Squeers lately occupied Dotheboys Hall, which had become a farm-house, and other relatives and descendants are respectable denizens of the vicinity. Dickens's exposure of the schools led to their extinction and to the consignment of Bowes to its present somnolent condition. In the village church-yard lie the lovers whose simultaneous deaths were commemorated by Mallet in "Edwin and Emma." At Barnard Castle, a few miles away, the prototype of Newman Noggs is still traditionally known, and known as "a gentleman."

The abounding beauties of the Greta have been painted by Turner and sung by Scott, both frequenters of this vale. From Bowes, a ramble along the lovely stream, between steep tree-shaded banks where it chafes and "greets" over the great rocks, and through mossy dells where it softly murmurs its content, brings us to the demesne of Rokeby, where Scott laid the scene of his famous poem. On every hand amid this region of enchantment, in glade and grove, in riven cliff and headlong torrent, in sunny slope and dingle's shade, we recognize the poetic imagery of Scott. Every turn reveals some new vista, rendered doubly delightful by the romantic associations with which the great poet has invested it. To the poet himself Greta's banks were potent allurements, and they were his habitual haunts during his sojourns in the valley. A descendant of the friend whom Scott visited here and to whom the poem is inscribed, points out to us a natural grotto, in the precipitous bank above the stream, where the poet often sat, and where some part of "Rokeby" was pondered and composed amid the scenery it portrays.

STERNE'S SWEET RETIRE-MENT

A T historic old York we are fairly in the
midst of great Yorkshire : standing upon
the tower of its colossal cathedral, we overlook
half that ancient county. At our feet lie the
quaint olden streets depicted in Collins's " No
Name," where erstwhile dwelt Porteus, Defoe,
Wallis, Lindley Murray, Mrs. Stannard, Poole of
" Synopsis Criticorum," Burton the author immortalized by Sterne as " Dr. Slop." Below us
we see the feudal castle where Eugene Aram was
hanged, the ancient city wall with its gate-ways
and battlements, the ruins of mediæval shrine
and of Roman citadel and necropolis ; abroad
we behold the vale which Bunsen pronounces
the " most beautiful in the world (the vale of
Normandy excepted)," with its streams, its
mosaics of green and golden fields and sombre
woods, its distant border of savage moors and
uplands. The Ouse, shining like a ribbon of
silver, flows at our feet ; we may trace its course
from the hills of Craven on the one hand,

while southward we behold it "slow winding through the level plain" on its way to the sea; into its valley we see the Wharfe flowing from the lovely dale where Collyer grew to manhood, and, farther away, the Aire emerging from the dreary region where lived the sad sisters Brontë and wove the sombre threads of their lives into romance.   The Foss flows toward us from the northeast, and our view along its valley embraces the region where dwelt Sydney Smith, while rising in the north are the Hambleton Hills, which shelter the vale where Sterne wrote the books that made him famous.   Indeed, this region of York is pervaded with memories of that prince of sentimentalists: in the great minster beneath us we find the tomb and monument of his grandfather, once archbishop of this diocese; in the carved pulpit of the minster Sterne preached as prebendary, and here he delivered his last sermon; his uncle was a dignitary of the old minster; his "indefatigably prolific" mother was native to this region; his wife was born here, and was first seen and loved by Sterne within sound of the glorious minster bells; most of his adult life was passed within sight of the minster towers.

At Sutton, Sterne's first living, the pilgrim finds little to reward his devotion.   Sterne's life here was obscure and, save in preparation, un-

productive. Skelton Castle was then the seat of
his college friend Stevenson, author of " Crazy
Tales," etc., who was the Eugenius of " Shandy,"
and to whom the " Sentimental Journey" was inscribed. Here Sterne found a library rich in rare
treatises upon unusual subjects, in which, during
his stay at Sutton, he spent much time and acquired a fund of odd and fanciful learning which
constituted in part his equipment for his work.
We find this castle nearer the stern coast which
Yorkshire opposes to the endless thunders of the
North Sea. Once a Roman stronghold, then a
feudal fortress and castle of the Bruces, later a
country-seat, it has since Sterne's time been rebuilt and modernized out of all semblance to the
" Crazy Castle" of his letters. It is believed
that only a few of the rooms remain substan-
tially as he knew them. A tradition is preserved
to the effect that during his visits here he bribed
the servants to tie the vane with the point
toward the west, because Eugenius would never
leave his bed while an east wind prevailed. A
near-by hill is called Sterne's Seat, but time has
left here little to remind us of the sentimental
" Yorick" who long haunted the place. It is
only at Coxwold, fourteen miles from York and
in the deeper depths of the shire, that we find
many remaining objects that were associated
with his work and with that portion of his life

which chiefly concerns the literary world. A result of the publication of the first part of " Tristram Shandy" was the presentation of this living to its author, and his removal to this sequestered retreat, which was to be his home during his too few remaining years. The hamlet has now a railway station, but the usual approach is by a rustic highway which conducts to and constitutes the village street. Within the hamlet we find a low-eaved road-side inn, and by it the shaded green where the rural festivals were held, and where, to celebrate the coronation of George III., Sterne had an ox roasted whole and served with great quantities of ale to his parishioners. Just beyond, Sterne's church stands intact upon a gentle eminence, overlooking a lovely pastoral landscape bounded by verdant hills. The church dates from the fifteenth century and is a pleasing structure of perpendicular Gothic style, with a shapely octagonal tower embellished with fretted pinnacles and a parapet of graceful design. One window has been filled with stained glass, but Sterne's pulpit remains, and the interior of the edifice is scarcely changed since he preached here his quaint sermons. The walls are plain ; the low ceiling is divided by beams whose intersections are marked by grotesque bosses ; the whole effect is depressing, and to the sensitive " Yorick"—haunted as he was by habitual dread that his ministrations might provoke a fatal pulmonary hemorrhage—it must have been dismal indeed. Among the effigied tombs of the Fauconbergs which line the chancel we find that of Sterne's friend who gave him this living.

Beyond the church and near the highway stands the quaint and picturesque old edifice where dwelt Sterne during the eight famous years of his life. In his letters he calls it Castle Shandy, and in all the countryside it is now known as Shandy Hall, shandy meaning in the local dialect crack-brained. It is a long, rambling, low-eaved fabric, with many heavy gables and chimneys, and steep roofs of tiles. Curious little casements are under the eaves; larger windows look out from the gables and are aligned nearer the ground, many of them shaded by the dark ivy which clings to the old walls and overruns the roofs. Abutting the kitchen is an astounding pyramidal structure of masonry—an Ailsa Craig in shape and solidity, yet more resembling Stromboli with its emissions of smoke,—which, beginning at the ground as a buttress, terminates as a kitchen-chimney and imparts to this portion of the house an architectural character altogether unique. Shrubbery grows about the old domicile, venerable trees which may have cast their shade upon " Yorick"

himself are by the door, and the aspect of the
place is decidedly attractive. To Sir George
Wombwell, who inherits the Fauconberg estate
through a daughter of Sterne's patron, we are
indebted for the preservation of the exterior of
the house in the condition it was when Sterne
inhabited it; but the interior has been parti-
tioned into two dwellings and thus considerably
altered. However, we may see the same
sombre wainscots and low ceiling that Sterne
knew, and we find the one room which interests us most—Sterne's parlor and study—little
changed. It is a pleasant apartment, with windows looking into the garden, where stood the
summer-house in which he sometimes wrote,
and beyond which was the sward where "my
uncle Toby" habitually demonstrated the siege
of Namur and Dendermond. On the low walls
of this room Sterne disposed his seven hundred
books,—"bought at a purchase dog-cheap,"—and
here he wrote, besides his sermons, seven volumes
of "Tristram Shandy" and the "Sentimental
Journey." There is a local tradition that other
MSS. written here were found by the succeed-
ing tenant and used to line the hangings of the
room. Sterne's letters afford glimpses of him
in this room: in one we see him "before the
fire, with his cat purring beside him;" in
another he is "sitting here and cudgelling his

brains" for ideas, though he usually wrote facilely and rapidly; in another he shows us a prettier picture, in which "My Lydia" (his daughter) "helps to copy for me, and my wife knits and listens as I read her chapters;" and later, after his estrangement from Mrs. Sterne, we see him "sitting here alone, as sad and solitary as a tomcat, which by the way is all the company I keep." In the repose of this charming place, and amid the peaceful influences about him here in his pretty home, Sterne appears at his best. And here for a time he was happy; we find his letters attesting, "I am in high spirits, care never enters this cottage;" "I am happy as a prince at Coxwold;" "I wish you could see in what a princely manner I live. I sit down to dinner—fish and wild fowl, or a couple of fowls, with cream and all the simple plenty a rich valley can produce, with a clean cloth on my table and a bottle of wine on my right hand to drink your health." But the melancholy days came all too soon; the "bursting of vessels in his lungs" became more and more frequent, his struggle with dread consumption was inaugurated, and now his letters from the pretty parsonage abound with references to his "vile cough, weak nerves, dismal headaches," etc. Now his "sweet retirement" has become "a cuckoldy retreat;" he complains of its situation, of its "death-doing, pestiferous wind." Returning to it from a sentimental journey or from a brilliant season of lionizing in London, he finds its quiet and seclusion insufferably irksome. Mortally ill, growing old, hopelessly estranged from his wife, deprived of the companionship of his idolized child, the poor master of Castle Shandy is "sad and desolate," his "pleasures are few," he sits "alone in silence and gloom." Such were some of the diverse phases of his life which these dumb walls have witnessed; in the dismalest, they have seen him at his desk here, resolutely ignoring his ills and tracing the passages of wit and fancy which were to delight the world. The incomplete "Sentimental Journey" was written in his last months of life.

A mile from Sterne's cottage, and approached by a way oft trodden by him and his "little Lyd," is Newburgh Hall, the ancient seat of Sterne's friend. Parts of the walls of a priory founded here in 1145 are incorporated into the oldest portion of the hall, and this has been added to by successive generations until a great, incongruous pile has resulted, which, however, is not devoid of picturesque beauty. Within this mansion Sterne was a familiar guest: urged by the friendly persistence of Fauconberg, he frequently came here to chat or dine with his friend and the guests of the hall, his brilliant converse making him the life of the company. Among the family portraits here are that of his benefactor and one of Mary Cromwell, wife of the second Fauconberg, who preserved here many relics of the great Protector, including his bones, which were somehow rescued from Tyburn and concealed in a mass of masonry in an upper apartment of the hall.

Sterne was not only popular with his lordly neighbor of Newburgh, but also, improbable as it would seem, with the illiterate yeomen who were his parishioners : although they understood not the sermons and found the sermonizer in most regards a hopeless enigma, yet, according to the traditions of the place, these simple folk discerned something in the complexly blended character of the creator of " my uncle Toby" which elicited their esteem and prompted many acts of love and service.   In a letter to an American friend, Arthur Lee, Sterne writes, " Not a parishioner catches a hare, a rabbit, or a trout, but he brings it an offering to me."

As set forth by the inscription at Sterne's cottage, he died in London.   One autumn day we find ourselves pondering the sad event of his last sojourn in the great city, as we stand upon the spot where his " truceless fight with disease" was ended, barely a fortnight after the " Sentimental Journey" was issued.   His wish to die " untroubled by the concern of his friends and the last service of wiping his brows and smoothing his pillow" was literally realized. During the publication of the "Journey" he lodged in rooms above a silk-bag shop in Old Bond Street; here he rapidly sank, and in the evening of March 18, 1768, attended only by a hireling who robbed his body, and in the presence of a staring footman, the dying man suddenly cried, " Now it is come !" and, raising his hand as if to repel a blow, expired. A few furlongs distant, opposite Hyde Park, we find an old cemetery hidden from the streets by houses and high walls which shut out the din of the great city. Here, in seclusion almost as complete as that of the graveyard of his own Coxwold, Sterne was consigned to earth. The spot is overlooked by the windows of Thackeray's sometime home. An old tree stands close by, and in its boughs the birds twitter above us as we essay to read the inscription which marks Sterne's poor sepulchre. But, mean and neglected as it is, we may never know that his ashes found rest even here; a report which has too many elements of probability and which never was disproved, avers that the grave was desecrated and that a horror-stricken friend recognized Sterne's mutilated corse upon the dissecting-table of a medical school. " Alas, poor Yorick !"

HAWORTH AND THE BRONTËS

OTHER Brontë shrines have engaged us,— Guiseley, where Patrick Brontë was married and Neilson worked as a mill-girl; the lowly Thornton home, where Charlotte was born; the cottage where she visited Harriet Martineau; the school where she found Caroline Helstone and Rose and Jessy Yorke; the Fieldhead, Lowood, and Thornfield of her tales; the Villette where she knew her hero; but it is the bleak Haworth hill-top where the Brontës wrote the wonderful books and lived the pathetic lives that most attracts and longest holds our steps. Our way is along Airedale, now a highway of toil and trade, desolated by the need of hungry poverty and greed of hungrier wealth: meads are replaced by blocks of grimy huts, groves are supplanted by factory chimneys that assoil earth and heaven, the once "shining" stream is filthy with the refuse of many mills. At Keighley our walk begins, and, although we have no peas in our "pilgrim shoon," the way is heavy with memories of the sad sisters Brontë who so often trod the dreary miles which bring us to Haworth. The village street, steep as a roof, has a pavement of rude stones, upon which the wooden shoes of the villagers clank with an unfamiliar sound. The dingy houses of gray stone, barren and ugly in architecture, are huddled along the incline and encroach upon the narrow street. The place and its situation are a proverb of ugliness in all the countryside; one dweller in Airedale told us that late in the evening of the last day of creation it was found that a little rubbish was left, and out of that Haworth was made. But, grim and rough as it is, the genius of a little woman has made the place illustrious and draws to it visitors from every quarter of the world. We are come in the "glory season" of the moors, and as we climb through the village we behold above and beyond it vast undulating sweeps of amethyst-tinted hills rising circle beyond circle,—all now one great expanse of purple bloom stirred by zephyrs which waft to us the perfume of the heather.

At the hill-top we come to the Black Bull Inn, where one Brontë drowned his genius in drink, and from our apartment here we look upon all the shrines we seek. The inn stands at the churchyard gates, and is one of the landmarks of the place. Long ago preacher Grimshaw flogged the loungers from its tap-room into chapel;

here Wesley and Whitefield lodged when holding meetings on the hill-top; here Brontë's predecessor took refuge from his riotous parishioners, finally escaping through the low casement at the back,—out of which poor Branwell Brontë used to vault when his sisters asked for him at the door. This inn is a quaint structure, low-eaved and cosy; its furniture is dark with age. We sleep in a bed once occupied by Henry J. Raymond, and so lofty that steps are provided to ascend its heights. Our meals are served in the old-fashioned parlor to which Branwell came. In a nook between the fireplace and the before-mentioned casement stood the tall arm-chair, with square seat and quaintly carved back, which was reserved for him. The landlady denied that he was summoned to entertain travellers here: " he never needed to be sent for, he came fast enough of himsel'." His wit and conviviality were usually the life of the circle, but at times he was mute and abstracted and for hours together " would just sit and sit in his corner there." She described him as a " little, red-haired, light-complexioned chap, cleverer than all his sisters put together. What they put in their books they got from him," quoth she, reminding us of the statement in Grundy's Reminiscences that Branwell declared he invented the plot and wrote the major part of " Wuthering

Heights." Certain it is he possessed transcending genius and that in this room that genius was slain. Here he received the message of renunciation from his depraved mistress which finally wrecked his life; the landlady, entering after the messenger had gone, found him in a fit on the floor. Emily Brontë's rescue of her dog, an incident recorded in "Shirley," occurred at the inn door.

The graveyard is so thickly sown with blackened tombstones that there is scant space for blade or foliage to relieve its dreariness, and the villagers, for whom the yard is a thoroughfare, step from tomb to tomb: in the time of the Brontës the village women dried their linen on these graves. Close to the wall which divides the church-yard from the vicarage is a plain stone set by Charlotte Brontë to mark the grave of Tabby, the faithful servant who served the Brontës from their childhood till all but Charlotte were dead. The very ancient church-tower still "rises dark from the stony enclosure of its yard;" the church itself has been remodelled and much of its romantic interest destroyed. No interments have been made in the vaults beneath the aisles since Mr. Brontë was laid there. The site of the Brontë pew is by the chancel; here Emily sat in the farther corner, Anne next, and Charlotte by the door, within a foot of the spot where her ashes now lie. A former sacristan remembered to have seen Thackeray and Miss Martineau sitting with Charlotte in the pew. And here, almost directly above her sepulchre, she stood one summer morning and gave herself in marriage to the man who served for her as " faithfully and long as did Jacob for Rachel." The Brontë tablet in the wall bears a uniquely pathetic record, its twelve lines registering eight deaths, of which Mr. Brontë's, at the age of eighty-five, is the last. On a side aisle is a beautiful stained window inscribed " To the Glory of God, in Memory of Charlotte Brontë, by an American citizen." The list shows that most of the visitors come from America, and it was left for a dweller in that far land to set up here almost the only voluntary memento of England's great novelist. A worn page of the register displays the tremulous autograph of Charlotte as she signs her maiden name for the last time, and the signatures of the witnesses to her marriage,—Miss Wooler, of " Roe Head," and Ellen Nussy, who is the E of Charlotte's letters and the Caroline of " Shirley."

The vicarage and its garden are out of a corner of the church-yard and separated from it by a low wall. A lane lies along one side of the church-yard and leads from the street to the vicarage gates. The garden, which was Emily's care, where she tended stunted shrubs and borders of unresponsive flowers and where Charlotte planted the currant-bushes, is beautiful with foliage and flowers, and its boundary wall is overtopped by a screen of trees which shuts out the depressing prospect of the graves from the vicarage windows and makes the place seem less "a church-yard home" than when the Brontës inhabited it. The dwelling is of gray stone, two stories high, of plain and sombre aspect. A wing is added, the little window-panes are replaced by larger squares, the stone floors are removed or concealed, curtains—forbidden by Mr. Brontë's dread of fire—shade the windows, and the once bare interior is furbished and furnished in modern style; but the arrangement of the apartments is unchanged. Most interesting of these is the Brontë parlor, at the left of the entrance; here the three curates of "Shirley" used to take tea with Mr. Brontë and were upbraided by Charlotte for their intolerance; here the sisters discussed their plots and read each other's MSS.; here they transmuted the sorrows of their lives into the stories which make the name of Brontë immortal; here Emily, "her imagination occupied with Wuthering Heights," watched in the darkness to admit Branwell coming late and drunken from the Black Bull; here Charlotte, the survivor of all, paced the night-watches in solitary anguish, haunted by the vanished faces, the voices forever stilled, the echoing footsteps that came no more. Here, too, she lay in her coffin. The room behind the parlor was fitted by Charlotte for Nichols's study. On the right was Brontë's study, and behind it the kitchen, where the sisters read with their books propped on the table before them while they worked, and where Emily (prototype of " Shirley"), bitten by a dog at the gate of the lane, took one of Tabby's glowing irons from the fire and cauterized the wound, telling no one till danger was past. Above the parlor is the chamber in which Charlotte and Emily died, the scene of Nichols's loving ministrations to his suffering wife. Above Brontë's study was his chamber; the adjoining children's study was later Branwell's apartment and the theatre of the most terrible tragedies of the stricken family; here that ill-fated youth writhed in the horrors of *mania-a-potu*; here Emily rescued him— stricken with drunken stupor—from his burning couch, as " Jane Eyre" saved Rochester; here he breathed out his blighted life erect upon his feet, his pockets filled with love-letters from the perfidious woman who wrought his ruin. Even now the isolated site of the parsonage, its environment of graves and wild moors, its exposure to the fierce winds of the long winters, make it unspeakably dreary; in the Brontë time it must have been cheerless indeed. Its influence darkened the lives of the inmates and left its fateful impression upon the books here produced. Visitors are rarely admitted to the vicarage; among those against whom its doors have been closed is the gifted daughter of Charlotte's literary idol, to whom "Jane Eyre" was dedicated, Thackeray.

By the vicarage lane were the cottage of Tabby's sister, the school the Brontës daily visited, and the sexton's dwelling where the curates lodged. Behind the vicarage a savage expanse of gorse and heather rises to the horizon and stretches many miles away: a path oft trodden by the Brontës leads between low walls from their home to this open moor, their habitual resort in childhood and womanhood. The higher plateaus afford a wide prospect, but, despite the August bloom and fragrance and the delightful play of light and shadow along the sinuous sweeps, the aspect of the bleak, treeless, houseless waste of uplands is even now dispiriting; when frosts have destroyed its verdure and wintry skies frown above, its gloom and desolation must be terrible beyond description. Remembering that the sisters found even these usually dismal moors a welcome relief from their tomb of a dwelling, we may appreciate the utter dreariness of their situation and the pathos of Charlotte's declaration, "I always dislike to leave Haworth, it takes so long to be content again after I return." We trace the steps of the Brontës across the moor to the cascade, called now the "Brontë Falls," where a brooklet descends over great boulders into a shaded glen. This was their favorite excursion, and as we loiter here we recall their many visits to the spot: first they came four children to play upon these rocks; later came three grave maidens with Caroline Helstone or Rose Yorke; later came two saddened women; and then Charlotte came alone, finding the moor a featureless wilderness full of torturing reminders of her dead, and seeing their vanished forms "in the blue tints, the pale mists, the waves and shadows of the horizon." Later still, during her few months of happiness, she came here many times with her husband, and her last walk on earth was made with him to see the cascade "in its winter wildness and power."

Above the village was the parsonage of Grimshaw and the original "Wuthering Heights." It was a sombre structure; a few trees grew about it, the moors rose behind; the apartments were like the oak-lined, stone-paved interior pictured in the tale, while the inscription above the door, H E 1659, was changed to Hareton

Earnshaw 1500 by Miss Brontë, who described
here much of her own grandfather's early life
and suffering and portrayed his wife in Catherine
Linton.   It is notable that the name Earnshaw
and other names in the Brontë books may be
seen on shop-signs along the way the sisters
walked to Keighley.

Among the villagers we meet some who remember the Brontës with affection and pride.
We find them so uniformly courteous that we
are willing to doubt Mrs. Gaskell's ascriptions
of surly rudeness.   They indignantly deny the
statements of Reid, Gaskell, and others regarding the character of Mr. Brontë.   One whose
relations to that clergyman entitle him to
credence assures us that Brontë did not destroy
his wife's silk dress, nor burn his children's
colored shoes, nor discharge pistols as a safety-
valve for his temper : " he didn't have that sort
of a temper."   It would appear that many
charges of the biographers were made upon the
authority of a peculating servant whom Brontë
had angered by dismissal.   Some parishioners
testify that " the Brontës had odd ways of
their own," " went their gait and didn't meddle
o'ermuch with us ;" " nobody had a word against
them."   Charlotte's husband, too, became popular after her death, perhaps at first because
of his tender care of her father : " to see the

good old man and Nichols together when the
rest were dead, and Mr. Brontë so helpless and
blind, was just a pretty sight." We hear more
than once of Brontë's wonderful cravat: he
habitually covered it himself, putting on new
silk without removing the old, until in the course
of years it became one of the sights of the
place, having acquired such phenomenal proportions that it concealed half his head. Many
still remember hearing him preach from the
depths of this cravat, while the sexton perambu-
lated the aisles with a staff to stir up the sleepers
and threaten the lads. Mr. Wood, a cabinet-
maker of the village, was church-warden in
Brontë's incumbency and an intimate friend of
the family till the death of the last member: his
loving hands fashioned the coffins for them all.
He was sent for to see Richmond's portrait of
Charlotte on its arrival, and was laughed at by
that lady for not recognizing the likeness; while
Tabby insisted that a portrait of Wellington,
which came in the same case, was a picture of
Mr. Brontë. That clergyman often complained
to Wood that Mrs. Gaskell "tried to make us
all appear as bad as she could." We find some
survivors of Charlotte's Sunday-school class
among the villagers. From one, who was also
singer in Brontë's church choir, we obtain
pictures of the church and rectory as they ap-

peared in Charlotte's lifetime and a photographic copy of Branwell's painting of himself and sisters, in which the likenesses are said to be excellent. Charlotte is remembered as being "good looking," having a wealth of lustrous hair and remarkably expressive eyes. She was usually neatly apparelled in black, and was so small that when Mrs. F. entered her class, at the age of twelve, the pupil was larger than the teacher. Another of Charlotte's class remembers her as being nervously quick in all her movements and a rapid walker; a third stood in the church-yard and saw her pass from the vicarage to the church on the morning of her marriage wearing a very plain bridal dress and a white bonnet trimmed with green leaves. A few brief months later this person, from the same spot, beheld the mortal part of her immortal friend borne by a grief-stricken company along the same path to her burial. In the hands of another of Charlotte's pupils we see a volume of the original edition of the poems of the three sisters, presented by Charlotte, and a Yorkshire collection of hymns which contains some of Anne's sweet verses.

It is evident that, of all the family, the hapless Branwell was most admired by the villagers. They delight to extol his pleasant manners, his ready repartee, his wonderful learning, his am-

Branwell Brontë—Brontë Relics

bidextrousness, his personal courage. On one
occasion restraint was required to prevent his
attacking alone a dozen mill-rioters, " any one of
whom could have put him in his pocket."
Holding a pen in each hand, he could simultaneously write letters on two dissimilar subjects
while he discoursed on a third. Wood thought
him naturally the brightest of the family, and
believed that lack of occupation, in a place
where there was nothing to stimulate mental
effort, accounted for his vices and failures. He
came often with his sisters to Wood's house, and
would talk by the hour of his projects to achieve
fame and fortune. One of his associates preserved some letters received from him while he
was "away tutoring," in which he shamelessly
recorded his follies and referred to himself as a
"Joseph in Egypt." A local society has col-
lected in its museum some Brontë mementos : a
relative of Martha, Tabby's successor in the
household, saved a few, — Charlotte's silken
purse, her thimble-case and some articles of
dress, elementary drawings made by the sisters,
autograph letters of Charlotte and her copies of
the " Quarterly" and other periodicals in which
she had read the reviews of "Jane Eyre."
Among the treasures Wood preserved were
sketches by Emily and Branwell ; a signatured
set of Brontë volumes presented by Brontë the

day before his death; Charlotte's worn history containing annotations in her microscopic chirography; a copy of "Jane Eyre" presented by Charlotte before its authorship was ascertained; an article on "Advantages of Poverty," by Mrs. Brontë; a highly graphic tale and religious poems by Mr. Brontë. Comment upon the latter reminded Wood that Brontë had shown him some poems by an Irish ancestor Hugh Brontë, and that he had met at the vicarage an irate relative who came from Ireland with a shillalah to "break the head" of a cruel critic of "Jane Eyre." Most of the Brontë belongings were removed by Mr. Nichols. He served the parish assiduously, as the people declare, for fifteen years, and at Brontë's death they desired that Nichols should succeed him; but the living was bestowed upon a stranger, and Nichols removed to the south of Ireland, where he married his cousin and is now a gentleman farmer. Martha Brown, the devoted servant of the family, accompanied him, and Nancy Wainwright, the Brontës' nurse, died some years ago in Bradford workhouse: so every living vestige of the family has disappeared from the vicinage.

A resident of near-by Wharfedale lately possessed a package of Charlotte's essays, written at the Brussels school and amended by "M. Paul." Study of these confirms the belief that

Charlotte Brontë's Husband

she was for a time tortured by a hopeless love for her preceptor, husband of "Madame Beck," and that it was this wretched passage in her life, rather than the fall of her brother, which "drove her to literary speech for relief." Her marriage with Nichols was eventually happy, but her own descriptions of him show that his were not the attributes that would please her fancy or readily gain her love. In "Shirley" she writes of him as successor of Malone: "the circumstance of finding himself invited to tea with a Dissenter would unhinge him for a week; the spectacle of a Quaker wearing his hat in church, the thought of an unbaptized fellow-creature being interred with Christian rites, these things would make strange havoc in his physical and mental economy." In a letter to E. Charlotte writes, "I am *not* to marry Mr. Nichols. I couldn't think of mentioning such a rumor to him, even as a joke. It would make me the laughing-stock of himself and fellow-curates for half a year to come. They regard me as an old maid, and I regard them, *one and all*, as highly uninteresting, narrow, and unattractive specimens of the coarser sex." Why then did she finally accept Mr. Nichols? Was it not from the same motive that had led her to reject his addresses not long before, the desire to please her father?

EARLY HAUNTS OF ROBERT COLLYER : EUGENE ARAM

THE factory-town of Keighley,—amid the moors of western Yorkshire,—to which the Brontë pilgrimage brings us, becomes itself an object of interest when we remember it was the birthplace of Robert Collyer. On a dingy side-street resonant with the din of spindles and looms and sullied with soot from factory chimneys, of humble parentage, and in a home not less lowly than that of another Yorkshire blacksmith in which Faraday was born, our orator and author first saw the light. Collyer came to Keighley "only to be born," and soon was removed to the lovely Washburndale, a few miles away. Here we find the place of the boyhood home he has made known to us—the cottage of two rooms with whitewashed walls and floor of flags—occupied by the mansion of a mill-owner, and the Collyer family vanished from the vicinage. "Little Sam," the kind-hearted father, fell dead at his anvil one summer day ; the blue-eyed, fair-haired mother, of whom the preacher so loves to speak, died in benign age; and the boisterous bairns who once filled the cottage are scattered in the Old World and the New. A little way down the sparkling burn is the picturesque old church of Fewston, where Collyer was christened, where Amos Barton of George Eliot's tale later preached, and where the poet Edward Fairfax—of the ancient family which gave to Virginia its best blood—was buried with his child who " was held to have died of witchcraft." Near by was Collyer's school, taught by a crippled and cross-eyed old fiddler named Willie Hardie, who survived at our first sojourn in the dale and had much to tell about his pupil " Boab," whom he had often " fairly thrashed." Collyer's school education ended in his eighth year, and he was early apprenticed at Ilkley, in the next valley, where he grew to physical manhood and attained to a measure of that intellectual stature which has since been recognized.

At Ilkley we find some who remember when Collyer came first, a stripling lad, to work in " owd Jackie's " smithy, and who in the long-ago worked, played, and fought with him in the village or read with him on the moors. One remembers that he was from the first an insatiable student, often reading, as he plied the bellows or switched the flies from a customer's horse. His master " Jackie " Birch, who was native of

A Literary Pilgrimage

Eugene Aram's home, is recalled as a selfish and
unpopular man, who had no sympathy with the
lad's studious habit, but tolerated it when it did
not interfere with his work. Collyer's love of
books was contagious, and soon a little circle of
lads habitually assembled, whenever released
from toil, to read with him the volumes borrowed
from friends or purchased by clubbing their own
scant hoards. A survivor of this group walked
with us through the village, pointing out the
spots associated with Collyer's life here, and
afterward showed us upon the slopes of the
overlooking hills the nooks where the lads read
together in summer holidays. Collyer was
especially intimate with the Dobsons : of these
John was best beloved, because he shared most
fully Collyer's studies and aspirations ; between
the two an affectionate friendship was formed
which, despite long separation and disparity of
position,—for John remained a laborer,—ended
only with his death. When, thirty years ago,
Collyer—honored and famous—revisited the
scenes of his early struggles and was eagerly invited to opulent and cultured homes, he turned
away from all to abide in the humble cottage of
Dobson, which we found near the site of the
smithy and occupied by others who were friends
of Collyer's youth. His associates of the early
time—some of them old and poor—tell us with

obvious pleasure and pride of his visits to their poor homes in these later summers when he comes to the place, and we suspect he often leaves with them more substantial tokens of his remembrance than kind words and wishes: indeed, he once made us his almoner to the more needy of them, one of whom we found in the workhouse. Some of his old-time friends recall the circumstances of his conversion under the preaching of a Wesleyan named Bland, his own eloquent and touching prayers, and his first timorous essays to conduct the services of the little chapel to which the villagers were bidden by the bellman, who proclaimed through the streets, " The blacksmith will preach t'night." When he preaches at Ilkley now, the Assembly-rooms are thronged with friends, old and new, eager to hear him. " Jackie" sleeps with his fathers, and the smithy is replaced by a modern cottage, into whose masonry many blackened stones from the old forge were incorporated. One of Collyer's chums showed us the door of the smithy which he had rescued from demolition and religiously preserved, and presented us with a photograph which we were assured represents the building just as Collyer knew it,—a long, low fabric of stone, with a shed joined at one end, two forge chimneys rising out of the roof, and the rough doors and window-shutters placarded with public notices. Before the forge was demolished, the large two-horned anvil on which Collyer wrought twelve years was bought for a price and removed to Chicago, where it is still preserved in the study of Unity Church, albeit Collyer long ago predicted to the writer, with a characteristic twinkle and a sweet hint of the dialect his tongue was born to, " they'll soon be sellin' *thet* for old iron."

The health-giving waters of the hill-sides attract hundreds of invalids and idlers, and the Ilkley of to-day is a smart town of well-kept houses, hotels, and shops, amid which we find here and there a quaint low-roofed structure which is a relic of the village of Collyer's boyhood. Among the survivals is the chapel—now a local museum, inaugurated by Collyer—where our " blacksmith" was converted and where he labored at the spiritual anvil as a local preacher. He has told us that for his labors in the Wesleyan pulpit during several years in Yorkshire and America he received in all seven dollars and fifty cents; he expounded for love, but pounded for a living. Another survival is the ancient parish church, built upon the site of the Roman fortress Olicana and of stones from its ruined walls, which preserves in its masonry many antiquarian treasures of Roman sculpture and inscription. Standing without are three curious monolithic columns, graven with mythological figures of men, dragons, birds, etc., which give them an archæological value beyond price. A doltish rector damaged them by using them as gate-posts; from this degradation the hands of Collyer helped to rescue them, and the same hands fashioned at the forge the neat iron gates which enclose the church-yard.

By the village and through the dale which Gray thought so beautiful flows the Wharfe; winding amid verdant meads, rushing between lofty banks, or loitering in sunny shallows, it holds its shining course to the Ouse, beyond the fateful field of Towton, where the red rose of Lancaster went down in blood. Ilkley nestles cosily at the foot of green slopes which swell away from the stream and are dotted with copses and embowered villas. Farther away the dim lines rise to the heights of the Whernside, whence we look to the chimneys of Leeds and the towers of York's mighty minster. Detached from Rumbald's cliffs lie two masses, called "Cow and Calf Rocks," bearing the imprint of giant Rumbald's foot: these rocks are a resort of the young people, and here Collyer and his friends oft came with their books. From this point Wharfedale, domed by a summer sky, seems a paradise of loveliness; its every aspect, from the glinting stream to the highest moorland crags, is replete with the beauty Turner loved to paint and which here first inspired his genius. Ruskin discerns this Wharfedale scenery throughout the great artist's works, bits of its beauty being unconsciously wrought into other scenes. These landscapes were a daily vision to the eyes of Collyer in the days when Turner still came to the neighborhood. This region abounds with memorials of the mighty past, with treasures of Druidical, Runic, and Roman history and tradition, but the literary pilgrim finds it rife with associations for him still more interesting: here lived the ancestors of our Longfellow, and the family whence Thackeray sprang; the fathers of that gentle singer, Heber, dwelt in their castle here and sleep now under the pavement of the church; a little way across the moors the Brontës dwelt and died. Here, too, lived the Fairfaxes,—one of them a poet and translator of Tasso,—and among their tombs we find that of Fawkes of Farnley, Turner's early friend and patron, while at the near-by hall are the rooms the painter occupied during the years he was transferring to canvas the beauties he here beheld. Farnley holds the best private collection of Turner's works, comprising, besides many finished pictures, numerous drawings and color-sketches made here.

A delightful excursion from Ilkley, one never

omitted by Collyer from his summer saunterings in Wharfedale, is to the sacred shades of Bolton Abbey. The way is enlivened with the prattle and sheen of the limpid Wharfe. A mile past the hamlet of Addingham, where Collyer preached his first sermon, the stream curves about a slight eminence which is crowned by the ruins of the ancient shrine. Some portions of the walls are fallen and concealed by shrubbery; other portions withstand the ravages of the centuries, and we see the crumbling arches, ruined cloisters, and mullioned windows, mantled with masses of ivy and bloom and set in the scene of restful beauty which Turner painted and Rogers and Wordsworth poetized. Our pleasure in the ruin and its environment of wood, mead, and stream is enhanced by the companionship of one who had, on another summer's day, explored the charms of the spot with George Eliot, and who repeats to us her expressions of rapturous delight at each new vista. Wordsworth loved this spot, and the incident to which the Abbey owed its erection—the drowning of young Romilly, the noble "Boy of Egremond," in the gorge near by—is beautifully told by him in the familiar poems written here.

Another excursion, by Knaresborough and the deadly field of Marston Moor, brings us into lovely Nidderdale, where stalks the dusky ghost of the Eugene Aram of Bulwer's tale and Hood's poem amid the scenes of his early life and of the crime for which he died. In the upper portion of the valley the Nidd winds like a ribbon of silver between green braes and moorland hills which rise steeply to the narrow horizon. From either side brooklets flow through wooded glens to join the wimpling Nidd, and at the mouth of one of these we find Ramsgill, where Aram was born. It is a straggling hamlet of thatched cottages, set among bowering orchards and gardens and wearing an aspect of tranquil comfort. The site of the laborer's hut in which the gentle student was born is shown at the back of one of the newer cottages of the place. Farther up the picturesque stream is the pretty village of Lofthouse, an assemblage of gray stone houses nestled beneath clustering trees, to which Aram returned after a short residence at Skipton, in the dale of the Brontës. Here he wooed sweet Annie Spence and passed his early years of married life; here his first children were born and one of them died. At the church in near-by Middlesmoor he was married; here his first child was christened, and in the bleak church-yard it was buried. Near a sombre "gill" which opens into the valley some distance below was Gowthwaite Hall, where Aram taught his first pupils,—an ancient, rambling structure of stone, two stories in height, with many steep gables and wide latticed windows. Venerable trees shaded the walls, leafy vines climbed to and overran the roofs, and a quaint garden of prim squares and formally trimmed foliage lay at one side. We found these externals little changed since Aram was tutor here. The partition of the mansion into three tenements had altered the arrangement of the interior, but the wide stairway still led from the entrance to the upper room at the east end, where Aram taught : it was a large, lofty apartment, reputed to be haunted, changed since his time only by the closing of one casement. Richard Craven was then tenant of the Hall, and his son, the erudite doctor, doubtless received his first tuition in this room and from Aram.

Some miles down the valley is Knaresborough, to which Aram removed from Lofthouse to establish a school, and where eleven years later the murder was committed. Soon after, Aram removed from the neighborhood, and during his residence at Lynn, where he was arrested for the crime, he was some time tutor in the house of Bulwer's grandfather, a circumstance which led to the production of the fascinating tale. A little way out of Knaresborough, in a recess at the base of the limestone cliffs which here border the murmuring Nidd, is the place where Clarke was killed and buried. This impressive spot was long the hermitage of " Saint Robert," who formed the cave out of the crag. In clearing the rubbish from the place after the publication of Bulwer's tale, the remains of a little shrine were found, and a coffin hewn from the rock, which proved that the hermitage had before been a place of burial, as urged by Aram in his defence. Upon a hill of the forest not far away the body of Aram hung in irons, and local tradition avers that his widow watched to recover the bones as they fell, and when she had at last interred them all, emigrated with her children to America.

It is noteworthy that belief in his innocence was universal among those who knew him in this countryside. Incidents illustrating his self-denial, patient forbearance, disregard for money, and care to preserve even the lowest forms of life are still cherished and recounted here as showing that robbery and murder were for him impossible crimes. We were reminded, too, that at the time of Clarke's disappearance Aram was husband of a woman of his own station, father of a family, and master of a moderately prosperous school,—conditions of which Bulwer could scarcely have been unaware, and which are inconsistent with the only motives

Belief in Aram's Innocence

suggested as inciting Aram to crime. In the opinion of the descendants of Aram's old neighbors in his native Nidderdale, Houseman was alone guilty ; and if Aram had, instead of undertaking to conduct his own defence, intrusted it to proper counsel, the trial would have resulted in his acquittal.

HOME OF SYDNEY SMITH

THE metropolis of England holds many
places which knew "the greatest of the
many Smiths:" dwellings he some time inhabited,
mansions in which he was the honored guest,
pulpits and rostrums from which he discoursed,
the room in which he died, the tomb where
loving hands laid him beside his son. But it is
in a remote valley of Yorkshire, where half his
adult years were passed in a lonely retreat among
the humble poor, that we find the scenes most
intimately associated with the fruitful period of
his life. In the lovely dale of York, not far
from one of the ancient gates and within sound
of the bells of the great minster, is the village
of Heslington, Smith's first place of abode in
Yorkshire. His dwelling here—lately the
rectory of a parish which has been created since
his time, and one of the best houses of the village
—is a spacious and substantial old-fashioned
mansion of brick, two stories in height and
delightfully cosy in appearance. Large bow-
windows, built by Smith, project from the front
and rise to the eaves. The rooms are of com-

fortable dimensions, and that in which Smith
wrote is "glorified" by the sunlight from one
of his great windows, near which his writing-
table was placed. The house stands a rod or
two from the highway, amid a mass of foliage;
an iron railing borders the yard, trees grow upon
either side, and at the back is an ample garden
which was Smith's especial delight, and which
he paced for hours as he pondered his compositions. It was here that the dignified Jeffrey of
the *Edinburgh Review* rode the children's pet
donkey over the grass. Smith's famous "Peter
Plimley" letters were produced at Heslington.
He never felt at home here, because he constantly
contemplated removing. His own parish had
no rectory, and he was permitted by his bishop
to reside here while he sought to exchange the
living for another : failing in this, he was allowed
a further term in which to erect a dwelling in
his parish, consequently Heslington was his
home for some years. During this time he
made weekly excursions to his church, twelve
miles distant, behind a steed which he commemorates as Peter the Cruel, and in the year he
built his parsonage the excursions were so
frequent that he computed he had ridden Peter
"several times round the world, going and
coming from Heslington."

In the remoter hamlet of Foston, "twelve

miles from a lemon," we find the church where
he ministered for twenty years and the house
which was his home longer than any other.
Our way thither—the same once so familiar to
Smith and his cruel steed—lies along the green
valley through which the wimpling Foss ripples
and sings on its way to the Ouse. In sun and
shadow our road leads through a pleasant country
until we see the roofs of Smith's parsonage
rising among the tree-tops. The Rector's Head,
as the wit delighted to call his home, stands
among the glebe-lands at a little distance from
the highway, and a carriage-drive—constructed
by Smith after some of his guests had been
almost inextricably mired in their attempts to
reach his door—conducts from a road-side gate
near the school through the tasteful and well-
kept grounds. Before we reach the rectory a
second barrier is encountered, Smith's " Screech-
ing Gate," which, like the gate at " Amen
Corner," remains just as it was when he bestowed its name. The mansion, of which he
was both architect and builder, described by him
and his friend Loch as " the ugliest house ever
seen," presents a singularly attractive aspect of
cosiness and comfort. The edifice is somewhat
improved since the great essayist dwelt beneath
its roof, but the original structure remains,—an
oblong brick fabric, of ample proportions and

unpretentious architecture, two stories in height, with hip-roofs of warm-tinted tiles. A large bay-window struts from one side wall; a beautiful conservatory abuts upon another side; a little porch, overgrown with creepers and flowers, protects the entrance. The once plain brickwork, which rose bare of ornamentation, is mantled with ivy and flowering vines which clamber to the roofs and riot along the walls, imparting to the "unparsonic parsonage" a picturesque charm which no architectural decoration could produce. The bare field in which Smith erected his house has been transformed into an Eden of beauty and bloom; on every side are velvety lawns, curving walks, beds of flowers, patches of shrubbery, and groups of woodland trees, forming a pretty park, mostly planned by Smith and planted by his hand. Within, we find the apartments spacious and cheerful: the windows are the same that were screened by the many-hued patchwork shades designed by Smith and wrought by the deft fingers of his daughters, the chimney-pieces of Portland stone which he erected remain, but tasteful and elegant furniture now replaces the rude handiwork of the village carpenter, which was disposed through these rooms during Smith's incumbency. He blithely tells a guest, "I needed furniture; I bought a cart-load of boards and got the carpenter, Jack Robinson; told him, 'Jack, furnish my house,' and you see the result." Some of the resulting furniture is still preserved in the neighborhood and valued above price. From the bay-window of the parlor the gray towers of York's colossal cathedral are seen ten miles away; the room adjoining at the left is the memorable apartment which was Smith's study, school-room, court, surgery, and what-not. Here his gayly-bound books were arranged by his daughter, the future Lady Holland, and here, when not applied to him, his famous "rheumatic armor" stood in a bag in yonder corner. Here he wrote his sermons, his brilliant and witty essays, the wise and effective disquisitions on the disabilities of the Catholics, the coruscating and incisive articles for the Review which electrified the English world. In this room he taught his children and gave Bible lessons to the youth of the parish, some of whom survive to praise and bless him; here, too, he prescribed for the sick and dispensed mercy rather than justice to culprits haled before him; for, as his letters declare, he was at once "village magistrate, village parson, village doctor, village comforter, and Edinburgh Reviewer." To these manifold avocations he added, despite his "not knowing a turnip from a carrot," that of the farmer, and managed the three hundred acres of glebe-lands

which were so unproductive that no one else
would cultivate them. A door-way of the rectory
overlooks most of the plantation, and he suspended here a telescope and a tremendous speak-
ing-trumpet by means of which he could observe and direct much of his operations without
himself going afield. Behind the house, and
screened by trees which Smith planted, are the
farmstead buildings he planned; here are the
stables and pens where he was welcomed by
every individual of his stock, whom he daily
visited to feed and pet; here is the enclosure
where he found his fuddled pigs "grunting God
save the King about the sty" after he had admin-
istered a medicament of fermented grains. In
the adjoining field is the site of his "Universal
Scratcher,"—a sharp-edged pole having a tall
support at one extremity and a low one at the
other, which so adapted it to the height of every
animal that "they could scratch themselves with
the greatest facility and luxury; even the
'Reviewer' [himself] could take his turn."

Of Smith's life in this retirement his many
letters and the memoirs of his daughter give us
pleasant pictures. Although he said his whole
life had "been passed like a razor, in hot water
or a scrape," the years spent here seem to have
been happy ones. Even his removal to this
house while it was yet so damp that the walls

ran down with wet and the grounds were so miry that his wife lost her shoes at the door, was made enjoyable. He writes to one friend, " I am too busy to be lonely ;" to another, " I thank God who made me poor that he also made me merry, a better gift than much land with a doleful heart ;" to another, " I am content and doubling in size every year ;" to Lady Grey, " Come and see how happy people can be in a small parsonage ;" to Jeffrey, " My situation is one of great solitude, but I possess myself in cheerfulness." He had expended upon his improvements here more than the living was worth, therefore economy ruled the selection of the *personnel* of this establishment. Faithful Annie Kay was first employed as child's-maid ; later she was housekeeper and trusted friend, removed from here with her loved master, attended him in his last illness, and lies near him in the long sleep. A garden girl, made like a mile-stone, was hired by Smith, who " christened her Bunch, gave her a napkin, and made her his butler." Jack Robinson was retained as general factotum of the place, and Molly Mills, " a yeowoman, with short petticoat, legs like mill-posts, and cheeks shrivelled like winter apples," did duty as " cow-, pig-, poultry-, garden-, and post-woman." Guests testify that good-natured training had, out of this unpromising material, produced such efficient servants that the household ran smoothly in the stress of much company. For, despite the seclusion of Smith's retreat, his fame and the charm and wit of his conversation drew many visitors to his house. Lords Carlisle and Morpeth were almost weekly guests; Sir Humphry Davy and his gifted wife were many times guests for days together; among those who came less frequently were Jeffrey, Macaulay, Marcet, Dugald Stewart, John Murray, Mackintosh, and Lord and Lady Holland, with many of less fame; and we may imagine something of the scintillant converse these rooms knew when the master wit entertained such company. Neither his friends nor his literary pursuits were allowed to interfere with his attentions to the simple rustics of his parish; in sickness and trouble he was tireless in their service, furnishing medicines, food, and clothing out of his slender means. During the prevalence of an infectious fever he was constantly among them, as physician, nurse, and priest. The oldest parishioners speak of him by his Christian name, and testify that he was universally beloved. One lately remembered that Sydney had cared for his father during a long illness and maintained the family until he could return to his work. Another had been accustomed, as a child, to run after Sydney on the highway and cling to him until he bestowed the sugar-plums he always carried in his pockets. In one portion of the glebe we found small enclosures of land stocked with abundant fruit-trees and called Sydney's Orchards, which were planted by him and given to the parishioners at a nominal rental.

Smith's solitary excursions through the parish were made astride a gaunt charger, called by him Calamity, noted for length of limb and strength of appetite, as well as for a propensity to part company with his rider, sometimes throwing the great Smith " over his head into the next parish." But when the rector's family were to accompany him, the ancient green chariot was employed. This was believed to have been the first vehicle of the kind, was purchased by Smith at second (or twenty-second) hand, and was from time to time partially restored by the unskilled village mechanics. Anent this structure the delightful Smith writes, " Each year added to its charms: it grew younger and younger: a new wheel, a new spring; I christened it the Immortal: it was known everywhere: the village boys cheered it, the village dogs barked at it." To the ends of the shafts Smith attached a rod so that it projected in front of the horse and sustained a measure of grain just beyond his reach,—a device which evoked a maximum of speed from the beast with the minimum of exertion on the part of the driver, the deluded horse being "stimulated to unwonted efforts by hope of overtaking the provender." We have talked with some in the vicinage who remembered seeing Smith and his family riding in this perennial chariot, drawn by a plough-horse which was harnessed with plough-lines and driven by a plough-boy.

A mile from the rectory, past the few straggling cottages of the hamlet, we come to the quaint little church of Foston, one of the oldest in England. It was already in existence in 1081 when Doomsday Book was compiled, being then the property of Earl Allen: later it was conveyed to St. Mary's Abbey, whose ruins—marvellously beautiful even in decay—we find at the gates of York. It is noteworthy that this church of Foston early contained an image of the Virgin of such repute that people flocked to it in great numbers, and in 1313 the archbishop issued an edict that they should not desert their own churches to come here. Smith's church is prettily placed upon a gentle eminence from which we look across a wave-like expanse of smiling fields to steeper slopes beyond, a picture of pastoral peace and calm. Beneath the many mouldering heaps of the church-yard sleep the rustic poor for whom Smith labored, many of them having been committed to their narrow cells, "in the certain hope of the life to come," by his kindly hands. Among the graves stands the old church, the plainest and smallest of its kind. The present venerable and reverend incumbent, to whom we are indebted for many courtesies, has at his own expense restored the chancel as a memorial of his wife, but the principal portion of the edifice remains the same "miserable hovel" that Macaulay described in Smith's day. A heavy porch shelters the entrance, and above this is a sculptured Norman arch of great antiquity, a Scripture subject being graven upon each stone, that upon the key-block representing the Last Supper. The bare walls are surmounted by a dilapidated belfry, and the barn-like edifice is desolate and neglected. We find the interior dismal and depressive, and quite unchanged since Smith's time, save that the stove-pipe now enters a flue instead of emerging through a window. The quaint old pulpit, perched high in the corner opposite the gallery and beneath a huge sounding-board, is the same in which he so often stood; its frayed and faded cushions are said to be those that he belabored in his discourses, and out of which, on one occasion, he raised such a cloud of dust "that for some minutes he lost sight of the congregation." The pewter communion plate he used is preserved in a recess of the wall. Across the

end and along one side of the church extends a
gallery, in which sat the children under Smith's
sharp eye, and kept in order, as some remember,
by "a threaten-shake of his head." Along the
front of this gallery ugly wooden pegs are aligned,
on which the occupants of the pews hang their
wraps, and so diminutive is the place that there
are but four pews between door and pulpit.
The present rector, whose father owned most
of the parish and was Smith's firm friend, attended as a boy Smith's ministrations here, and
remembers something of the direct eloquence
of his sermons and their impressive effect upon
the auditors. Attracted by his fame, some came
from far to hear him preach who afterward
became his ardent friends, among these being
Macaulay and the Mrs. Apreece whom de Staël
depicted as "Corinne" and who subsequently,
as wife of Humphry Davy, was guest at The
Rector's Head. In this shabby little church
Smith gave away his daughter Emily, the Archbishop of York reading the marriage service;
and not long after Smith removed to Somerset,
and Foston saw him no more.

The church contains no memorial of any sort
in memory of Smith. The decayed condition
of this temple has long been a reproach to the
resident gentry. Since those whose property
interests are most concerned in the restoration

of the church have declined to enter upon it, the good rector contemplates undertaking it at his own charge. Not long ago he was engaged upon the plans, and it may be that, by the time these pages reach the reader, Foston church as Smith knew it will have ceased to exist. The writer has a lively hope that some of the New World pilgrims who have marked other Old World shrines which else had been neglected, will set in these renovated walls an enduring memorial—of pictured glass or sculptured stone or graven metal—in remembrance of the illustrious author-divine who, during his best years, ministered in this lowly place to a congregation of rude and unlettered poor.

NITHSDALE RAMBLES

FROM the " Heart of Mid-Lothian" and the many shrines of picturesque Edinburgh, once the literary capital of Britain, our saunterings bring us to other haunts of the " Wizard of the North :" to his oft described Abbotsford, —that baronial " romance in stone and lime,"— with its libraries and armories, its precious relics and more precious memories of its illustrious builder and occupant, who here literally " wrote himself to death ;" to the dream-like, ivy-grown ruins of holy Melrose, whose beauties he sang and within whose crumbling walls he lingered and mused ; to his tomb fittingly placed amid the ruined arches and mouldering pillars of Dryburgh Abbey, embowered by venerable trees and mantled by clinging vines. Strolling thence among the " Braes of Yarrow," the Yarrow of Wordsworth and Hamilton, through the haunts of Hogg the Ettrick Shepherd, and passing the Hartfell, we come into the dale of Annan, and follow that winsome water past Moffat, where lived Burns's daughter, to historic Applegarth, and thence by Lockerby approach

A Literary Pilgrimage

Ecclefechan, the hamlet of Carlyle's birth and sepulture. Among the lowly stone cottages on the straggling street of the rude village is a double dwelling with an arched passage-way through the middle of its lower story; this humble structure was erected by the stone-mason James Carlyle, and the northern end of it was his home when his illustrious son was born. Opening from the street is a narrow door; beside it is a diminutive window, with a similar one above and another over the arch. The exterior is now smartened somewhat,—the shillings of pilgrims would pay for that,—but the abode is pathetically small, bare, and poor. The one lower room is so contracted that the Carlyles could not all sit at the table, and Thomas used to eat his porridge outside the door. Some Carlyle relics from Cheyne Row—letters, portraits, pieces of china, study-lamp, tea-caddy, and other articles—are preserved in the room above, and adjoining it is the narrow chamber above the archway where the great historian, essayist, and cynic was born. In this comfortless home, and amid the dreary surroundings of this hard and rough village, which is little improved since the days of border war and pillage, he was reared. The stern savagery of the physical horizon of his boyhood here, and the hateful and uncongenial character of his environment at the most impressionable period of his life, may account to us for much of the morose cynicism of his later years. Further excuse for his petulance and his acerbities of tongue and temper is found in his dyspepsia, and a very limited experience of Ecclefechan cookery suffices to convince us that his indigestion was another unhappy sequence of his early life in this border hamlet. In "Sartor Resartus" he has vivaciously recorded some of the incidents and impressions of his childhood here,—notably the passage of the Carlisle coach, like "some terrestrial moon, coming from he knew not where, going he knew not whither." A shabby cross-street leads to the village graveyard, which was old a thousand years ago, and there, within a few rods of the spot of his birth, the great Carlyle is forever laid, with his parents and kindred. The yard is a forlorn enclosure, huddled with hundreds of unmarked graves, and with other hundreds of crumbling memorials drooping aslant among the brambles which infest the place. The tombstone of Carlyle, within an iron railing, is a little more pretentious than those about it, but his grave seems neglected; daisies and coarse grass grow about it, and the only tokens of reverent memory it bears are placed by Americans, who constitute the majority of the pilgrims to this place. Not far from the kirk-yard is a lowly cottage, hardly better than a hut, in which dwelt Burns's " Lass of Ecclefechan."

By a transverse road from Lockerby we come to the ruined Lochmaben Castle of Bruce, and thence into Nithsdale and to Dumfries, the ancient capital of southwestern Scotland. Here lived Edward Irving, and here Allan Cunningham toiled as a common mason ; but the gray town is interesting to us chiefly because of its associations with Burns. Here are the tavern, familiar to us as the " howff," which he frequented, and where he made love to the barmaid, " Anna of the Gowden Locks ;" the parlor where his wit kept the table in a roar ; the heavy chair in the " ingle neuk" where he habitually sat, and, in the room above, the lines to " Lovely Polly Stewart" graven by his hand upon the pane. From the inn a malodorous lane, named Burns Street, and oft threaded by the bard when he " wasna fou but just had plenty," leads to the poor dwelling where lived and died the poet of his country and of mankind. An environment more repulsive and depressing, a spot more unworthy to be the home of a poet of nature, can scarcely be imagined. Here not a flower nor a green bough, not even a grass-blade, met his vision, not one beautiful object appeased his poetic taste ; he saw only the squalid street infested by unwashed bairns and bordered by rows of mean cottages. How shall we extol the genius which in such an uncongenial atmosphere produced those exquisite poems which for a century have been read and loved in every clime? His own dwelling, a bare two-storied cottage, is hardly more decent than its neighbors. Within, we find a kitchen and sitting-room, small and low-ceiled; above, a windowed closet,—sometimes used by the poet as a study,—and the poor little chamber where he died, only thirty-seven years after he first saw the light in the clay biggin by his bonnie Doon.

The interior of St. Michael's Church has been refitted, and the sacristan can show us now only the site of Burns's seat, behind a great pillar which hid him from the preacher, and that of the Jenny on whose bonnet he saw the " crowlin' " pediculus. Through the crowded church-yard a path beaten by countless pilgrims from every quarter of the globe conducts to the place where he lies with "Bonnie Jean" and some of their children. The costly mausoleum which now covers his tomb—erected by those who had neglected or shunned him in his life— is to us less impressive than the poor little gravestone which the faithful Jean first placed above him, which now forms part of the pavement.

A Literary Pilgrimage

The ambitious statue, designed to represent Genius throwing her mantle over Burns at the plough, suggests, as some one has said, that a bath-woman bringing a wet sheet to an unwilling patient had served as a model. Oddly enough, the grave of John Bushby, an attorney oft lampooned in Burns's verse, lies but a few feet from that of the poet.

Our ramble along the wimpling Nith lies for the most part in a second Burnsland, so closely is it associated with his personality and poetry. The beauties of the stream itself are celebrated in half a score of his songs. Every seat and scene are sung in his verse; every neighborhood and almost every house preserve some priceless relic or some touching reminiscence of the ploughman-bard. A short way above Dumfries we come to the picturesque ruin of Lincluden Abbey, at the meeting of the waters of Cluden and Nith. The crumbling walls are enshrouded in ivy and surrounded by giant trees, among which Burns loved to loiter. His " Evening View" and " Vision" commemorate this ruin, and the poem " Lincluden" was written here. In a tasteful cottage not far from the Abbey sojourned the Mrs. Goldie who communicated to Scott the incidents which he wrought into his " Heart of Mid-Lothian," and it was in the little kitchen of this cottage that the lady talked

Jeanie Deans—Carlyle's Craigenputtock

with Helen Walker, the original Jeanie Deans. In a poor little low-eaved dwelling, a mile or two up the valley, that heroine lived, keeping a dame's school and rearing chickens; and our course along the tuneful stream brings us to the ancient and sequestered kirk-yard of Irongray, where, among the grass-grown graves of the Covenanters, her ashes repose beneath a tomb-stone erected by Scott himself and marked by an inscription from his hand: "Respect the Grave of Poverty when associated with love of Truth and dear Affection." Farther in this lovely region we come to ancient Dunscore and the monument of Scott's "Old Mortality;" and beyond Moniaive we find, near the source of the Cairn, Craigenputtock—the abode where "Thomas the Thunderer prepared his bolts" before he removed to London. This dreary place, "the loneliest in Britain," had been the abode of many generations of Mrs. Carlyle's ancestors,—among whom were "several black-guards but not one blockhead,"—and Carlyle rebuilt and furnished the house here to which he brought the bride he had wedded after his repulsion by his fair Rose-goddess, the Blumine of his "Romance." It is a severely plain and substantial two-storied structure of stone with steep gables. The entrance is under a little porch in the middle of the front; on either side is a single window, with another above it in the second story. There are comfortable and commodious rooms at each side of the entrance, and a large kitchen is joined at the back. Carlyle's study, a rather sombre apartment, with a dispiriting outlook, is at the left; a fireplace which the sage especially loved is in one wall, his writing-table stood near it, and here he sat and clothed in virile diction the brilliant thoughts which had come to him as he paced among his trees or loitered on the near hill-tops. The dining-room and parlor are on the other side, looking out upon wild and gloomy crags. Mrs. Carlyle's pen long ago introduced us to this interior, and, although all her furniture, except perhaps the kitchen "dresser," has been removed, we recognize the household nooks she has mentioned. The kitchen, which was the scene of her tearful housekeeping trials, seems most familiar; its chimney retains its abominable habits, but a recent incumbent, instead of crying as did Mrs. Carlyle, declared the "chimla made her feel like sweerin'." Great ash-trees, which were old when the sage dwelt beneath them, overtop the house; many beautiful flowers—some survivors of those planted by Carlyle and his wife—bloom in the yard. In front a wide field slopes away to a tributary of the Cairn, but sombre moorland hills rise at the back and cluster close about the house on either side, imparting to the place an indescribably depressing aspect : as we contemplate the desolate savagery of this wilderness, we can understand why one of Carlyle's predecessors here killed himself and others " took to drink."

The bare summit behind the house overlooks Carlyle's estate of a thousand acres and, beyond it, an expanse of bleak hills and black morasses. From the craggy brow on the left, the spot where Carlyle and Emerson sat and talked of the immortality of the soul, we see Dunscore and a superb vista of the valley towards Dumfries and the Wordsworth country. The isolation of this place—so complete that at one time not even a beggar came here for three months—was an advantage to Carlyle at this period. He speaks of it as a place of plain living and high thinking : life here appeared to him " an humble russet-coated epic," and long afterward he referred to the years of their stay in this waste as being " perhaps the happiest of their lives." This expresses his own feeling rather than that of his wife, whose discontent finds expression in many ways, notably in her poem " To a Swallow." Carlyle produced here some of his best work, including the matchless " Sartor Resartus," the essay on Burns, and several scintillant articles for the various reviews which denoted the rise of a new star of genius; but the period of his stay here was essentially one of study and thought, and, plenteous as it was in production, it was more prolific in preparation for the great work he had to do. To Carlyle in this solitude Jeffrey was a visitor, as well as "Christopher North," Hazlitt, and Edward Irving: hither, "like an angel from heaven," came Emerson to greet the new genius on the threshold of its career and to enjoy the "quiet night of clear, fine talk." Carlyle bequeathed this estate to the University of Edinburgh.

Another day, our ramble follows the winding Nith northward from Lincluden. As we proceed, the lovely and opulent dale, once the scene of clannish strife, presents an appearance of peaceful beauty, pervaded everywhere with the sentiment of Burns. In one enchanting spot the stream circles about the grounds of ancient Friars Carse, now a tasteful and pretty seat. It was erstwhile the residence of Burns's friend Riddel, to which the poet was warmly welcomed: here he composed the poem "Thou whom Chance may hither lead," and here he presided at the famous drinking-match which he told to future ages in "The Whistle." It is noteworthy that the first Scotch winner of the Whistle was father of Annie Laurie of the popular song, and that the contest here was between two of her grandnephews and her grandson,—the latter being victorious. Burns celebrated his friend of this old hermitage in seven of his poems; and the present proprietor carefully cherishes the window upon whose pane the bard inscribed "Lines written in Friars Carse." A little way beyond lies Druidical Holywood, where once dwelt the author of "De Sphæra," and next we find the Nith curving among the acres which Burns tilled in his happiest years, at Ellisland. Embowered in roses and perched upon an eminence overhanging the stream is the plain little dwelling which he erected with his own hands for the reception of his bonnie Jean. It is little changed since the time he lived under its lowly roof. We think the rooms dingy and bare, but they are better than those of his abode at Alloway and Mossgiel, much better than those in which he died at Dumfries. In the largest of the apartments, by a window which looks down the dreamful valley, Burns had a rude table, and here he penned some of the most touchingly beautiful poetry of our language,—poems which he had pondered as he worked or walked afield. Adjoining the house is the yard where he produced the exquisite lines "To Mary in Heaven;" in this near-by field he met "The Wounded Hare" of his verse; in yonder path along the murmuring Nith he composed the immortal " Tam O'Shanter," laughing aloud the while at the pictures his fancy conjured ; and all about us are reminders of the bard and of the idyllic life which here inspired his muse : it would repay a longer journey to see the spot where the one song " John Anderson, my Jo" was pondered and written.

A further jaunt amid varied beauties of woodland shade and meadow sunshine, of gentle dale and savage scaur, brings us past historic Closeburn to the neighborhood of Thornhill. Here at the Buccleuch Arms the illegitimate daughter of Burns was for thirty years a servant, and boasted of having had a chat with Scott among the burnished utensils of her kitchen. Two miles eastward Scott found the Balfour's Cave and Leap described in " Old Mortality." Middle Nithsdale expands into a broad valley, commanded by lofty Queensberry and lower green hills and diversified with upland brae, shadowy copse, sunny mead, and opulent plantation. This lovely region, dotted with pretty hamlets, embowered villas, and moss-grown ruins, and teeming with the charming associations of history and sentiment, holds for us a crowning interest which has drawn our steps into its romantic haunts : it was the birthplace and life-long home of Annie Laurie. On the right of the Nith, among the bonnie braes of the song, we find the ancient

manor-house of Maxwelton, where the heroine
was born. The first of her race to reside here
was her great-grandfather, who in 1611 built
additions to the old tower already existing.
The marriage-stone of Annie Laurie's grand-
parents, John Laurie and Agnes Grierson, is
set in the massive walls and graven with their
initials, crest, and date. This Agnes was
daughter of the bloody persecutor who figures in
" Redgauntlet," and whose ashes lie in Dunscore
kirk-yard, not far distant. Another stone in the
Maxwelton house commemorates the marriage
of Robert Laurie and Jean Riddel, the parents
of the heroine of the song,—this Robert being
the champion of Bacchus who won the Whistle
from the noble Danish toper. In this ancient
abode, according to a record made by her father,
" At the pleasure of the Almighty God, my
daughter Anna Laurie was born upon the 16th
day of Decr., 1682 years, about six o'clock
in the morning ;" here the bonnie maiden grew
to womanhood ; here occurred the episode to
which the world is indebted for the sweet song ;
from here she married and went to her future
home, but a few miles away. In the last century much of the venerable edifice was destroyed,
but the older portion, which had been part of a
stronghold in the time of the border wars, remains
intact since Annie dwelt within. This part is

still called The Tower, and consists of a large
rectangular structure, with a ponderous semi-
circular fabric abutting it at one end, its fortress-
like walls being five feet in thickness and clothed
by a luxuriant growth of ivy. Newer portions
have been added in varying styles, and the mansion is now an elegant and substantial seat. All
about it lie terraced lawns, with parterres of
flowers, noble trees, and banks of shrubbery:
lovely grounds slope away from the house and
command an enchanting view which must often
have delighted the vision of the fair Annie.
Her boudoir is in the second story of The
Tower; it is a corner room, forming now an
alcove of the drawing-room; it has a vaulted
ceiling of stone, and its windows, pierced in the
ponderous walls, look out through the ivy and
across an expanse of sward, flower, and foliage
to the wooded braes where she kept tryst with
her lover. Among the treasures of the old
house is a portrait of the bonnie heroine which
shows her as an impressively beautiful woman,
of lissome figure, large and tender eyes, long
oval face with Grecian features, wide forehead
framed by a profusion of dark-brown hair. Her
hands, like her " fairy feet," were of exceptional
smallness and beauty. The present owner of
Maxwelton, to whom the writer is indebted for
many courtesies, is Sir Emilius Laurie; from

him and from the lineal descendants of the widely-sung Annie who still inhabit Nithsdale are derived the materials for this account of that winsome lady. The lover who immortalized her was William Douglas of Fingland, and she requited him by breaking " her promise true" and marrying another man. Douglas is said to have been the hero of the song " Willie was a Wanton Wag ;" he was one of the best swordsmen of his time, and his personal qualities gained him the patronage of the Queensberry family and secured him social advantages to which his lower rank and poverty constituted no claim. He and Annie met at an Edinburgh ball, and seem to have promptly become enamoured of each other. To separate them, Sir Robert quickly carried his family back to Nithsdale, but Douglas as quickly followed, and lurked in the vicinage for some months, clandestinely meeting his love among " Maxwelton's bonnie braes." Here the pair plighted troth, and when Douglas returned to Edinburgh, to assist in a projected Stuart uprising, he took with him the promise which he celebrated in the tender melody. The song was published in an Edinburgh paper and attracted much notice. Douglas's devotion to the Jacobites cost him his sweetheart; his political intrigues being suspected, he was forced to fly the country, and when, after some years passed in

France, he secured pardon and returned, she was the wife of another. After giving "her promise true" to some other lovers, she married in 1709 Alexander Fergusson, a neighboring laird, who could not write poetry but had "muckle siller an' lan'" and a genealogy as long as Leviticus. Douglas and Annie never met again, and she makes but a single reference to him in her letters: being told of his return, she wrote to her sister, Mrs. Riddel, grandmother of Burns's friend, "I trust he has forsaken his treasonable opinions and is content."

A stroll of but a few miles along a delightful way, fanned by the sweet summer winds, brings us to Craigdarrock, Annie Laurie's home for more than half a century. It is a spacious and handsome edifice of three stories, with dormer-windows in the hip-roof; a conservatory is connected at one end, bow-windows project from either side, and clambering vines cover the walls of the lower stories.

It is beautifully placed in a vale overlooking the winding stream, with the rugged Craigdarrock looming steeply in the background. Most of the mansion was built under the direction of Annie Laurie, and the gardens were laid out by her in their formal style: a delightful walk beneath the trees on the margin of the water was her favorite resort, and is still known by her

HOME OF ANNIE LAURIE.

…an·e, he …… … … and returned, she …… the w… … … … After giving " her promise fr… … … …her lovers, she married in 170) … … …ergusson, a neighboring laird, w… … …t write poetry but had " muck'… … … …" " and a genealogy as long as Levit… … … …as and Annie never met again, a… … … … but a single reference to him in h… … … …ng told of his return, she wrote t… …er sister, M… R…d…l, grandmother of Burns's friend, " I trust … …has …rsaken his treasonable opinions and is content."

… … … … … …

… … … … … …

… … … …us and

… … …, with dormer-windows … … … … con ervatory is conne… … …, …ow-windows project from e… … … …clamb…ng vines cover the walls o… … …storie·

It is … …ly place… in a vale overlooking the windin… …am, with the rugged Craigdarrock loomin… …eply i… the background. Most of the ma… …a was …uilt under the direction of Annie …ie, and the gardens were laid out by …r in …r formal style: a delightful w… …neath …ees on th… margin of the w… …… …rt, a… is still k… …… …wr

name. Within the spacious rooms are preserved
many of her belongings : curious furniture and
hangings, quaint fineries of dress, her porcelain
snuff-box, her will, a package of her letters
written in the prim fashion of her time and
signed " Anna." Through these epistles we
look in vain for indications of the wit and genius
which one naturally attributes to the possessor
of the bright face which inspired a deathless
song. In this house she lived happily with her
husband, and was at once the Lady Bountiful and
the matchmaker-in-ordinary for the whole
countryside ; here she died, aged seventy-nine.
This estate has been handed down from father
to son for fifteen generations, the present urbane
laird, Captain Cutlar Fergusson, being a great-
great-grandson of Annie Laurie and grandson
of the hero of Burns's " Whistle." This famous
trophy—a plain object in dark wood—is preserved here at Craigdarrock, and has not been
challenged for since the bout which Burns
witnessed.

In the now ruined church of Glencairn,
hardly a mile from her birthplace, and not far
from her later home, Annie Laurie worshipped,
and in its yard, which has been a place of burial
for a thousand years, she was laid with her husband, among the many generations of his kindred,
by the gable-end of the ancient church. Her

sepulchre was not marked, and it is to be feared the bones of the erst beauteous lady have been more than once disturbed in excavating for later interments in the crowded plot. From the summit of Craigdarrock we look upon the wilder beauty of the upper Nith, a region of moorland hills and dusky glens, where we may find the birthplace of " the Admirable Crichton," and beyond it the bleak domain where the poet Allan Ramsay first saw the light. Beyond this, again, the sweet Afton " flows amang its green braes," and we come to the Ayrshire shrines of Burns.

A few miles westward from Craigdarrock, and not so far from Carlyle's lonely den, is Fingland farm, the birthplace and home of Annie's poet-lover. It lies among sterile hills in the wild Glenkens of ancient Galloway, near the source of Ken water. From neighboring elevations we see Craigenputtock and the swelling Sol-way, and westward we look, across the dark fens and heathery hills of the region " blest with the smell of bog-myrtle and peat," al-most to the Irish Sea. In this region Crockett was reared, and he pictures it in his charm-ing tales " The Raiders" and " The Lilac Sun-bonnet."

No trace of the peel-tower in which Douglas dwelt remains, but we know that it stood within an enclosing wall twenty yards square and one yard in thickness. The tower had projecting battlements; its apartments, placed above each other, were reached by a narrow, easily defended stair. In such a home and amid this most dismal environment Douglas grew to manhood, his poetic power unsuspected until it was called forth by the love and beauty of Annie Laurie. Later he wrote many poems, but diligent inquiry among the families of Buccleuch and Queensberry shows that few of his productions are now extant save the famous love-song. It is notable that he did not "lay doun his head and die" for the faithless Annie; instead, he made a runaway marriage with Elizabeth Clerk, of Glenborg, in his native Galloway, subsided into prosy country life, and reared a family of six children, of whom one, Archibald, rose to the rank of lieutenant-general in Brittany.

Douglas's song was revised by Lady Scott, sister of the late Duke of Buccleuch, and published by her for the benefit of the widows and orphans made by the Crimean War. Lines of the original, for which the writer is indebted to a descendant of Annie Laurie, are hereto appended, that the reader may appreciate how much of the tender beauty of the popular version of the song is attributable to the poetic talent of Lady Scott.

A Literary Pilgrimage

" Maxwelton banks are bonnie,
    Where early fa's the dew,
Where me and Annie Laurie
    Made up the promise true :
Made up the promise true,
    And ne'er forget will I :
And for bonnie Annie Laurie
    I'd lay doun my head and die.

" She's backit like a peacock ;
    She's breastit like a swan ;
She's jimp about the middle ;
    Her waist ye weel may span :
Her waist ye weel may span,—
    She has a rolling eye ;
And for bonnie Annie Laurie
    I'd lay doun my head and die."

A NIECE OF ROBERT BURNS

*Her Burnsland Cottage—Reminiscences of Burns—Relics—Por-
traits—Letters—Recitations—Account of his Death—Memories of his Home—Of Bonnie Jean—Other Heroines.*

IN the course of a summer ramble in Burnsland we had sought out the homes, the
haunts, the tomb of the ploughman poet, and had
bent at many a shrine hallowed by his memory
or his song. From the cottage of "Bonnie
Jean" and the tomb of "Holy Willie," the field
of the "Mountain Daisy" and the church of the
"Holy Fair," the birthplace of "Highland
Mary" and the grave of "Mary Morison," we
came to the shrines of auld Ayr, beside the sea.
Here we find the "Twa Brigs" of his poem ; the
graves of the ministers satirized in "The Kirk's
Alarm ;" the old inn of "Tam O'Shanter," and
the very room, with its ingle, where Tam and
Souter Johnny "got fou thegither," and where
we may sip the nappy from the wooden caup
which Tam often drained. From Ayr a delightful stroll along the highway where Tam made
his memorable ride, and where William Burns
carried the howdie upon the pillion behind him
on another stormy winter's night when the poet
was born, brought us to the hamlet of Alloway
and the place of Burns's early life. Here are the
auld clay biggin, with its rude stone floor and

roof of thatch, erected by the unskilled hands of his father, where the poet first saw the light, and where he laid the scene of the immortal "Cotter's Saturday Night;" the fields where his young hands toiled to aid his burdened sire; the kirk-yard where his kindred lie buried, some of their epitaphs written by him; the "auld haunted kirk,"—where Tam interrupted the witches' dance,—unknown save for the genius of the lad born by its roofless walls; the Burns monument, with its priceless relics; the ivy-grown bridge, four centuries old, whose arch spans the songful stream and across which Tam galloped in such sore peril, and its "key-stane," where Meg lost "her ain gray tail" to Nannie, fleetest of the pursuers; the enchanting "banks and braes of bonnie Doon," where Burns wandered a brown-eyed boy, and later found the inspiration of many of his exquisite strains. We have known few scenes more lovely than this in which his young life was passed: long and delightful is our lingering here, for interwoven with the many natural beauties are winsome memories of the bard whose spirit and genius pervade all the scene.

Returning thence past the "thorn aboon the well" (the well is closed now) and the "meikle-stane" to the ancient ford "where in the snaw the chapman smoor'd," we made a détour southward, and came by a pleasant way—having in view on the right the picturesque ruin of Greenan Castle upon a cliff overhanging the sea—to Bridgeside cottage, the home of Miss Isabella Burns Begg, niece of the poet and long his only surviving near relative. We found a cottage of stone, from whose thatched roof a dormer-window, brilliant with flowers, peeped out through the foliage which half concealed the tiny homelet. The trimmest of little maids admitted us at the gate and led along a path bordered with flowers to the cottage door, where stood Miss Begg beaming a welcome upon the pilgrims from America. We were ushered into a prettily furnished little room, upon whose walls hung a portrait of Burns, one of his sister Mrs. Begg, and some framed autograph letters of the bard, which the niece "knew by heart." She was the daughter and namesake of Burns's youngest and favorite sister, who married John Begg. We found her a singularly active and vivacious old lady, cheery and intelligent, and more than pleased to have secured appreciative auditors for her reminiscences of her gifted uncle. She was of slender habit, had a bright and winning face, soft gray hair partially concealed by a cap, and when she was seated beneath the Burns portrait we could see that her large dark eyes— now sparkling with merriment or misty with emotion, and again literally glowing with feeling —were like those on the canvas. Among the treasures of this room was a worn copy of Thomson's " Seasons," a favorite book of Burns, which he had freely annotated; his name in it is written " Burnes," as the family spelled it down to the publication of the bard's first volume. In the course of a long and pleasant chat we learned that Miss Begg had lived many years in the cottage, first with her mother and later with her sister Agnes,—named for Burns's mother,—who died before our visit and was laid beside her parents and the father of Burns in the kirk-yard of auld Alloway, where Miss Begg expected " soom day, please God an it be soon," to go to await the resurrection, thinking it an " ill hap" that she survived her sister. She innocently inquired if we " kenned her nephew Robert in America," and then explained that he and a niece of hers had formerly lived with her, but she had discovered that " they were sweetheartin' and wantin' to marry, which she wouldna allow, so they went to America," leaving her alone with her handmaiden. Most of her visitors had been Americans. She remembered the visits of Hawthorne, Grant, Stanley, and Helen Hunt Jackson,—the last with greatest pleasure,—and thought that " Americans care most about Burns." She mentioned the visit

of a Virginian maid, who by rapturous praise
of the uncle completely won the heart of the
niece. The fair enthusiast had most of Burns's
poems at her tongue's end, but insisted upon
having them repeated by Miss Begg, and at
parting exclaimed, after much kissing, " Oh,
but I always pray God that when he takes me
to heaven he will give me the place next to
Burns." Apparently, Robin still has power to
disturb the peace of " the lasses O." Yet we
can well excuse the effusiveness of our com-
patriot: to have listened to the old lady as she
sat under his portrait, her eyes twinkling or
softening like his own, her voice thrilling with
sympathetic feeling as she repeated in his own
sweet dialect the tender stanzas, " But pleasures
are like poppies spread," " My Mary! dear departed shade!" and " Oh, happy love, when
love like this is found," and others of like pathos
and beauty, is a rapture not to be forgotten.
She spoke quickly, and the Scottish accent kept
one's ears on the alert, but it rendered the lines
doubly effective and melodious. Many of the
poems were inspired by special events of which
Miss Begg had knowledge from her mother,
which she recalled with evident relish. She
distinctly remembered the bard's widow, " Bonnie Jean," and often visited her in the poor
home where he died. Jean had a sunny tem-

per, a kind heart, a handsome figure, a fine voice, and lustrous eyes, but her brunette face was never bonnie. While she lacked intellectual appreciation of his genius, she was proud of and idolized him, finding ready excuse and forgiveness for his failings. When the frail "Anna with the Gowden Locks" bore him an illegitimate child, Jean cradled it with her own, and loyally averred to all visitors, "It's only a neebor's bairn I'm bringin' up." ("Ay, she must 'a' lo'ed him," was Miss Begg's comment on this part of her narrative.) Jean had told that in his last years the poet habitually wore a blue coat, with nankeen trousers (when the weather would allow), and his coat-collar was so high that his hat turned up at the back. Her account of the manner of his death is startling, and differs from that given by the biographers. He lay apparently asleep when "sweet Jessy"—to whom his last poem was written—approached, and, to remind him of his medicine, touched the cup to his lips; he started, drained the cup, then sprang headlong to the foot of the bed, threw his hands forward like one about to swim, and, falling on his face, expired with a groan. Jean saw him for the last time on the evening before his funeral, when his wasted body lay in a cheap coffin covered with flowers, his care-worn face framed by the wavy masses of his sable hair, then sprinkled with gray. At his death he left MSS. in the garret of his abode, which were scattered and lost because Jean was unable to take care of them,—a loss which must ever be deplored.

One of the delights of Miss Begg's girlhood was the converse of Burns's mother concerning her first-born and favorite child, the poet, a theme of which she never tired. Miss Begg remembered her as a "chirk" old lady with snapping black eyes and an abundant stock of legends and ballads. She used to declare that Bobbie had often heard her sing "Auld Lang Syne" in his boyhood; hence it would appear that, at most, he only revised that precious old song. Miss Begg more than once heard the mother tell, with manifest gusto, this incident of their residence at Lochlea. Robert was al-ready inclined to be wild, and between visiting his sweetheart Ellison Begbie—"the lass of the twa sparkling, roguish een"—and attending the Tarbolton club and Masonic lodge was abroad until an unseemly hour every night, and his mother or Isabella sat up to let him in. His anxious sire, the priest-like father of the "Cotter's Saturday Night," determined to administer an effectual rebuke to the son's misconduct, and one night startled the mother by announcing significantly that he would wait to admit the lad. She lay for hours (Robert was later than ever that night), dreading the encounter between the two, till she heard the boy whistling "Tibbie Fowler" as he approached. Then the door opened: the father grimly demanded what had kept him so late; the son, for reply, gave a comical description of his meeting auld Hornie on the way home,—an adventure narrated in the "Address to the De'il,"—and next the mother heard the pair seat themselves by the fire, where for two hours the father roared with laughter at Robert's ludicrous account of the evening's doings at the club,—she, meanwhile, nearly choking with her efforts to restrain the laughter which might remind her husband of his intended reproof. Thereafter the lad stayed out as late as he pleased without rebuke. The niece had been told by her mother that Burns was deeply distressed at his father's death-bed by the old man's fears for the future of his wayward son; and when his father's death made Robert the head of the family, he every morning led the household in "the most beautiful prayers ever heard;" later, at Ellisland and elsewhere, he continued this practice, and on the Sabbath instructed them in the Catechism and Confession. Mrs. Begg's most pleasing recollections of her brother were associated with the farm-life at Mossgiel, where he so far gave her his confidence that she was allowed to see his poems in the course of their composition. He would ponder his stanzas during his labors afield, and when he came to the house for a meal he would go to the little garret where he and his brother Gilbert slept and hastily pen them upon a table which stood under the one little window. Here Isabella would find them, and, after repeated perusals, would arrange them in the drawer; and so it passed that her bright eyes were the first, besides his own, to see " The Twa Dogs," " Winter's Night," " The Bard's Epitaph," " The Cotter's Saturday Night," the satirical poems, and most of the productions which were published in his Kilmarnock volume. His sister testified that he was always affectionate to the family, and that after his removal to a home of his own he invariably brought a present for each when he revisited the farm, the present for his mother being always, despite his poverty, a costly pound of tea. Most of the receipts from his publishers were given to the family at Mossgiel. Miss Begg intimated that Burns's mother did not at first like his wife, because of the circumstances of the marriage, but Jean's stanch devotion to her husband won the heart of the doting mother, and they became warm friends and spent much time together after Burns's death. The niece believed that the accounts of his intemperance are mostly untrue. Her mother, who was twenty-five years old at the time of his decease, always asserted that she " never saw him fou," and believed it was his antagonism to the " unco' guid" that made them ready to believe and circulate any idle report to his discredit.

Mrs. Begg saw and liked " Highland Mary" at the house of Gavin Hamilton, and knew Miss Dunlop, the blooming Keith of Burns's " New-Year Day." Another of his heroines the niece had herself visited with her mother ; this was Mrs. Jessy Thompson, *née* Lewars, who was a ministering angel in his final illness, and was repaid by the only thing he could bestow,—a song of exquisite sweetness, " Here's a health to ane I lo'e dear." Our informant had seen in that lady's hands the lines beginning " Thine be the volumes, Jessy fair," which the poet gave her with a present of books within a month of his death. Many other reminiscences related by the niece are to be found in the biographies of the bard, and need not be repeated. The letters which hung upon her walls are not included in any published collection. She assisted us in copying the following to Burns's youngest brother :

A Letter of Burns

" ISLE, Tuesday Evening.

"DEAR WILLIAM, — In my last I recom-
mended that valuable apothegm, Learn taciturn-
ity. It is certain that nobody can know our
thoughts, and yet, from a slight observation of
mankind, one would not think so. What mischiefs daily arise from silly garrulity and foolish
confidence! There is an excellent Scots saying
that a man's mind is his kingdom. It is certainly so, but how few can govern that kingdom
with propriety! The serious mischiefs in Busi-
ness which this Flux of language occasions do
not come immediately to ycur situation, but in
another point of view—the dignity of man—
now is the time that will make or mar. Yours
is the time of life for laying in habits. You
cannot avoid it, tho' you will choose, and these
habits will stick to your last end. At after-
periods, even at so little advance as my years,
'tis true that one may still be very sharp-sighted
to one's habitual failings and weaknesses, but to
eradicate them, or even to amend them, is quite
a different matter. Acquired at first by accident, they by-and-by begin to be, as it were, a
necessary part of our existence. I have not
time for more. Whatever you read, whatever
you hear of that strange creature man, look into
the living world about you, look to yourself, for

the evidences of the fact or the application of
the doctrine.   I am ever yours,

"ROBERT BURNS.

"MR. WILLIAM BURNS, Saddler, Longtown."

The sentiment and style of this epistle are
suggestive of the stilted conversations of Burns,
recorded in Hugh Miller's "Recollections."
Miss Begg was pleased by some account we could
give her of American Burns monuments and festivals; she seemed reluctant to have us leave,
called to us a cheery "God keep ye!" when we
were without the gate, and stood looking after
us until the intervening foliage hid her from our
sight.   As we walked Ayr-ward, while the sun
was setting in a golden haze behind the hills of
Arran, we felt that we had been very near to
Burns that day,—had almost felt the thrill of his
presence, the charm of his voice, and had in
some measure made a personal acquaintance with
him which would evermore move us to a tenderer regard for the man and a truer appreciation
of his verse, as well as a fuller charity for his
faults:

We know in part what he has done,
God knows what he resisted.

For some months after our visit to Bridgeside,
quaint letters—one of them containing a portrait of the worthy occupant of the cottage—

followed us thence across the sea.   These came at increasing intervals and then stopped; the kindly heart of the niece of Burns had ceased to beat on her eightieth birthday.

A recent pilgrim in Burnsland found an added line on the gravestone in the old kirk-yard, to tell that Isabella Burns Begg rests there in eternal peace.   At Bridgeside, her once cherished garden is a waste and her tiny cottage has wholly disappeared.   " So do things pass away like a tale that is told."

HIGHLAND MARY: HER HOMES AND GRAVE

Birthplace – Personal Appearance – Relations to Burns – Abodes: Mauchline, Coilsfield, etc.–Scenes of Courtship and Parting – Mementos – Tomb by the Clyde.

THERE is no stronger proof of the transcending power of the genius of Burns than is found in the fact that, by a bare half dozen of his stanzas, an humble dairy servant—else unheard of outside her parish and forgotten at her death—is immortalized as a peeress of Petrarch's Laura and Dante's Beatrice, and has been for a century loved and mourned of all the world. We owe much of our tenderest poesy to the heroines whose charms have attuned the fancy and aroused the impassioned muse of enamoured bards; readers have always exhibited a natural avidity to realize the personality of the beings who inspired the tender lays,—prompted often by mere curiosity, but more often by a desire to appreciate the tastes and motives of the poets themselves. How little is known of Highland Mary, the most famous heroine of modern song, is shown by the brief, incoherent, and often contradictory allusions to her which the biographies of the ploughman-poet contain. This paper, —prepared during a sojourn in " The Land o' Burns,"—while it adds a little to our meagre

knowledge of Mary Campbell, aims to present
consecutively and congruously so much as may
now be known of her brief life, her relations to
the bard, and her sad, heroic death.

She first saw the light in 1764, at Ardrossan,
on the coast, fifteen miles northward from the
"auld town of Ayr." Her parentage was of the
humblest, her father being a sailor before the
mast, and the poor dwelling which sheltered her
was in no way superior to the meanest of those
we find to-day on the narrow streets of her village. From her birthplace we see, across the
Firth of Clyde, the beetling mountains of the
Highlands, where she afterward dwelt, and
southward the great mass of Ailsa Craig looming, a gigantic pyramid, out of the sea. Mary
was named for her aunt, wife of Peter McPher-
son, a ship-carpenter of Greenock, in whose
house Mary died. In her infancy her family
removed to the vicinage of Dunoon, on the
western shore of the Firth, eight miles below
Greenock, leaving the oldest daughter at Ardrossan. Mary grew to young womanhood
near Dunoon, then returned to Ayrshire, and
found occupation at Coilsfield, near Tarbolton,
where her acquaintance with Burns soon began.
He told a lady that he first saw Mary while
walking in the woods of Coilsfield, and first
spoke with her at a rustic merry-making, and,

"having the luck to win her regards from other suitors," they speedily became intimate. At this period of life Burns's "eternal propensity to fall into love" was unusually active, even for him, and his passion for Mary (at this time) was one of several which engaged his heart in the interval between the reign of Ellison Begbie—"the lass of the twa sparkling, roguish een"—and that of "Bonnie Jean." Mary subsequently became a servant in the house of Burns's landlord, Gavin Hamilton, a lawyer of Mauchline, who had early recognized the genius of the bard and admitted him to an intimate friendship, despite his inferior condition. When Hamilton was persecuted by the kirk, Burns, partly out of sympathy with him, wrote the satires, "Holy Willie's Prayer," "The Twa Herds," and "The Holy Fair," which served to unite the friends more closely, and brought the poet often to the house where Mary was an inmate. This house—a sombre structure of stone, little more pretentious than its neighbors—we found on the shabby street not far from Armour's cottage, the church of "The Holy Fair," and "Posie Nansie's" inn, where the "Jolly Beggars" used to congregate. Among the dingy rooms shown us in Hamilton's house was that in which he married Burns to "Bonnie Jean" Armour.

The bard's niece, Miss Begg, of Bridgeside,

told the writer that she often heard Burns's mother describe Mary as she saw her at Hamilton's: she had a bonnie face, a complexion of unusual fairness, soft blue eyes, a profusion of shining hair which fell to her knees, a *petite* figure which made her seem younger than her twenty summers, a bright smile, and pleasing manners, which won the old lady's heart. This description is, in superlative phrase, corroborated by Lindsay in Hugh Miller's " Recollections:" she was " beautiful, sylph-like," her bust and neck were " exquisitely moulded," her arms and feet " had a statue-like symmetry and marble-like whiteness ;" but it was in her lovely countenance that " nature seemed to have exhausted her utmost skill,"—" the loveliest creature I have ever seen," etc. All who have written of her have noticed her beauty, her good sense, her modesty and self-respect. But these qualities were now insufficient to hold the roving fancy of Burns, whose " susceptibility to immediate impressions" (so called by Byron, who had the same failing) passes belief. His first ephemeral fancy for Mary took little hold upon his heart, and the best that can be said of it is that it was more innocent than the loves which came before and after it. Within a stone's-throw of Mary dwelt Jean Armour, and when the former returned to Coilsfield, he promptly fell in love with Jean, and solaced himself with her more buxom and compliant charms. It was a year or so later, when his intercourse with Jean had burdened him with grief and shame, that the tender and romantic affection for Mary came into his life. She was yet at Coilsfield, and while he was in hiding—his heart tortured by the apparent perfidy of Jean and all the country-side condemning his misconduct—his intimacy with Mary was renewed; his quickened vision now discerned her endearing attributes, her trust and sympathy were precious in his distress, and awoke in him an affection such as he never felt for any other woman. During a few brief weeks the lovers spent their evenings and Sabbaths together, loitering amid the

> " Banks and braes and streams around
> The castle of Montgomery,"

talking of the golden days that were to be theirs when present troubles were past; then came the parting which the world will never forget, and Mary relinquished her service and went to her parents at Campbeltown,—a port of Cantyre behind " Arran's mountain isle." Of this parting Burns says, in a letter to Thomson, " We met by appointment on the second Sunday of May, in a sequestered spot on the Ayr, where we spent the day in taking farewell before she should embark for the West Highlands to prepare for our projected change of life." Lovers of Burns linger over this final parting, and detail the impressive ceremonials with which the pair solemnized their betrothal : they stood on either side of a brook, they laved their hands in the water and scattered it in the air to symbolize the purity of their intentions ; clasping hands above an open Bible, they swore to be true to each other forever, then exchanged Bibles, and parted never to meet more. It is not strange that when death had left him nothing of her but her poor little Bible, a tress of her golden hair, and a tender memory of her love, the recollection of this farewell remained in his soul forever. He has pictured it in the exquisite lines of " Highland Mary" and " To Mary in Heaven."

In the monument at Alloway—between the " auld haunted kirk" and the bridge where Maggie lost her tail—we are shown a memento of the parting ; it is the Bible which Burns gave to Mary and above which their vows were said. At Mary's death it passed to her sister, at Ardrossan, who bequeathed it to her son William Anderson ; subsequently it was carried to America by one of the family, whence it has been recovered to be treasured here. It is a pocket edition in two volumes, to one of which is attached a lock of poor Mary's shining hair.

A Literary Pilgrimage

Within the cover of the first volume the hand of Burns has written, " And ye shall not swear by my name falsely, I am the Lord;" within the second, " Thou shalt not forswear thyself, but shalt perform unto the Lord thine oaths." Upon a blank leaf of each volume is Burns's Masonic signet, with the signature, " Robert Burns, Mossgiel," written beneath. Mary's spinning-wheel is preserved in the adjoining cottage. A few of her bright hairs, severed in her fatal fever, are among the treasures of the writer and lie before him as he pens these lines.

A visit to the scenes of the brief passion of the pair is a pleasing incident of our Burns-pilgrimage. Coilsfield House is somewhat changed since Mary dwelt beneath its roof,—a great rambling edifice of gray weather-worn stone with a row of white pillars aligned along its façade, its massive walls embowered in foliage and environed by the grand woods which Burns and Mary knew so well. It was then a seat of Colonel Hugh Montgomerie, a patron of Burns. The name Coilsfield is derived from Coila, the traditional appellation of the district. The grounds comprise a billowy expanse of wood and sward; great reaches of turf, dotted with trees already venerable when the lovers here had their tryst a hundred years ago, slope away from the mansion to the Faile and border its murmuring course to the Ayr. Here we trace with romantic interest the wanderings of the pair during the swift hours of that last day of parting love, their lingering way 'neath the " wild wood's thickening green," by the pebbled shore of Ayr to the brooklet where their vows were made, and thence along the Faile to the woodland shades of Coilsfield, where, at the close of that winged day, "pledging oft to meet again, they tore themselves asunder." Howitt found at Coilsfield a thorn-tree, called by all the country " Highland Mary's thorn," and believed to be the place of final parting; years ago the tree was notched and broken by souvenir seekers; if it be still in existence the present occupant of Coilsfield is unaware.

At the time of his parting with Mary, Burns had already resolved to emigrate to Jamaica, and it has been supposed, from his own statements and those of his biographers, that the pair planned to emigrate together; but Burns soon abandoned this project and, perhaps, all thought of marrying Mary. The song commencing " Will ye go to the Indies, my Mary ?" has been quoted to show he expected her to accompany him, but he says, in an epistle to Thomson, that this was his farewell to her, and in another song, written while preparing to embark, he declares that it is leaving Mary that makes him wish to tarry. Further, we find that with the first nine pounds received from the sale of his poems he purchased a single passage to Jamaica,—manifestly having no intention of taking her with him. Her being at Greenock in October, *en route* to a new place of service at Glasgow, indicates she had no hope that he would marry her then, or soon. True, he afterward said she came to Greenock to meet him, but it is certain that he knew nothing of her being there until after her death. During the summer of 1786, while she was preparing to wed him, he indited two love-songs to her, but they are not more glowing than those of the same time to several inamoratas,—less impassioned than the "Farewell to Eliza" and allusions to Jean in "Farewell, old Scotia's bleak domains,"—and barely four weeks after his ardent and solemn parting with Mary we find him writing to Brice, "I do still love Jean to distraction." Poor Mary! Possibly the fever mercifully saved her from dying of a broken heart. The bard's anomalous affectional condition and conduct may perhaps be explained by assuming that he loved Mary with a refined and spiritual passion so different from his love for others—and especially from his conjugal love for Jean—that the passions could coexist in his heart. The alternative explanation is that his love for Mary, while she lived, was by no means

the absorbing passion which he afterward believed it to have been. When death had hallowed his memories of her love and of all their
sweet intercourse,—beneficent death ! that beau-
tifies, ennobles, irradiates, in the remembrance
of survivors, the loved ones its touch has taken,
—then his soul, swelling with the passion that
throbs in the strains of " To Mary in Heaven,"
would not own to itself that its love had ever
been less.

Mary remained at Campbeltown during the
summer of 1786. Coming to Greenock in the
autumn, she found her brother sick of a malig-
nant fever at the house of her aunt; bravely
disregarding danger of contagion, she devoted
herself to nursing him, and brought him to a
safe convalescence only to be herself stricken by
his malady and to rapidly sink and die, a sacrifice
to her sisterly affection. By this time the suc-
cess of his poems had determined Burns to remain in Scotland, and he returned to Mossgiel,
where tidings of Mary's death reached him.
His brother relates that when the letter was
handed to him he went to the window to read
it, then his face was observed to change suddenly, and he quickly went out without speaking. In June of the next year he made a solitary journey to the Highlands, apparently drawn
by memory of Mary. If, indeed, he dropped

a tear upon her neglected grave and visited her humble Highland home, we may almost forgive him the excesses of that tour, if not the renewed *liaison* with Jean which immediately preceded, and the amorous correspondence with "Clarinda" (Mrs. M'Lehose) which followed it.

Whatever the quality or degree of his passion for Mary living, his grief for her dead was deep and tender, and expired only with his life. Cherished in his heart, it manifested itself now in some passage of a letter, now in some pathetic burst of song,—like "The Lament" and "Highland Mary,"—and again in some emotional act. Of many such acts narrated to the writer by Burns's niece, the following is, perhaps, most striking. The poet attended the wedding of Kirstie Kirkpatrick, a favorite of his, who often sang his songs for him, and, after the wedded pair had retired, a lass of the company, being asked to sing, began "Highland Mary." Its effect upon Burns "was painful to witness; he started to his feet, prayed her in God's name to forbear, then hastened to the door of the marriage-chamber and entreated the bride to come and quiet his mind with a verse or two of 'Bonnie Doon.'" The lines "To Mary in Heaven" and the pathetic incidents of their composition show most touchingly how he mourned his fair-haired lassie years after she ceased to be. It was at Ellisland, October 20, 1789, the anniversary of Mary's death, an occasion which brought afresh to his heart memories of the tender past. Jean has told us of his increasing silence and unrest as the day declined, of his aimless wandering by Nithside at nightfall, of his rapt abstraction as he lay pillowed by the sheaves of his stack-yard, gazing entranced at the " lingering star" above him till the immortal song was born.

Poor Mary is laid in the burial-plot of her uncle in the west kirk-yard of Greenock, near Crawford Street; our pilgrimage in Burnsland may fitly end at her grave. A pathway, beaten by the feet of many reverent visitors, leads us to the spot. It is so pathetically different from the scenes she loved in life,—the heather-clad slopes of her Highland home, the seclusion of the wooded braes where she loitered with her poet-lover. Scant foliage is about her; few birds sing above her here. She lies by the wall; narrow streets hem in the enclosure; the air is sullied by smoke from factories and from steamers passing within a stone's-throw on the busy Clyde; the clanging of many hammers and the discordant din of machinery and traffic invade the place and sound in our ears as we muse above the ashes of the gentle lassie.

A Literary Pilgrimage

For half a century her grave was unmarked and neglected; then, by subscription, a monument of marble, twelve feet in height, and of graceful proportions, was raised. It bears a sculptured medallion representing Burns and Mary, with clasped hands, plighting their troth. Beneath is the simple inscription, read oft by eyes dim with tears:

Erected Over the Grave of
HIGHLAND MARY
1842.
" My Mary, dear departed shade,
Where is thy place of blissful rest ?"

BRONTË SCENES IN BRUS-
SELS

School-Class-Rooms-Dormitory-Garden-Scenes and Events of Villette and The Professor-M. Paul-Madame Beck-Memories of the Brontës-Confessional-Grave of Jessy Yorke.

W E had " done" Brussels after the approved
fashion,—had faithfully visited the
churches, palaces, museums, theatres, galleries,
monuments ; had duly admired the windows and
carvings of the grand cathedral, the tower and
tapestry and frescos and façade of the Hôtel de
Ville, the stately halls and the gilded dome of
the Courts of Justice, and the consummate beauty
of the Bourse ; had diligently sought out the
naïve boy-fountain, and had made the usual excursion to the field of Waterloo.

This delightful task being conscientiously
discharged, we proposed to devote our last day in
the Belgian capital to the accomplishment of one
of the cherished projects of our lives,—the searching out of the localities associated with Charlotte
Brontë's unhappy school-life here, which she
has so graphically portrayed. For our purpose
no guide was needful, for the topography and
local coloring of " Villette" and " The Professor" are as vivid and unmistakable as in the best
work of Dickens himself. Proceeding from St.

Gudule to the Rue Royale, and a short distance along that thoroughfare, we reached the park and a locality familiar to Miss Brontë's readers. Seated in this lovely pleasure-ground, the gift of the Empress Maria Theresa, with its cool shade all about us, we noted the long avenues and the paths winding amid trees and shrubbery, the dark foliage ineffectually veiling the gleaming statuary and the sheen of bright fountains, "the stone basin with its clear depth, the thick-planted trees which framed this tremulous and rippled mirror," the groups of happy people filling the seats in secluded nooks or loitering in the mazes and listening to the music; we noted all this, and felt that Miss Brontë had revealed it to us long ago. It was across this park that Lucy Snowe was piloted from the bureau of the diligence by the chivalrous Dr. John on the night when she, despoiled, helpless, and solitary, arrived in Brussels. She found the park deserted, the paths miry, the water dripping from the trees. "In the double gloom of tree and fog she could not see her guide, and could only follow his tread" in the darkness. We recalled another scene under these same trees, on a night when the gate-way was "spanned by a flaming arch of massed stars." The park was a "forest with sparks of purple and ruby and golden fire gemming the foliage," and Lucy, driven from her couch by mental torture, wandered unrecognized amid the gay throng at the midnight concert of the Festival of the Martyrs and looked upon her lover, her friends the Brettons, and the secret junta of her enemies, Madame Beck, Madame Walravens, and Père Silas. The sense of familiarity with the vicinage grew as we observed our surroundings. Facing us, at the extremity of the park, was the palace of the king, in the small square across the Rue Royale at our right was the statue of General Béliard, and we knew that just behind it we should find the Brontë school; for " The Professor," standing by the statue, had looked down a great staircase to the door-way of the school, and poor Lucy on that forlorn first night in "Villette," to avoid a pair of ruffians, had hastened down a flight of steps from the Rue Royale and had come, not to the inn she sought, but to the *pensionnat* of Madame Beck. From the statue we descended, by a series of stone stairs, into a narrow street, old-fashioned and clean, quiet and secluded in the very heart of the great city, and just opposite the foot of the steps we came to the wide door of a spacious, quadrangular, stuccoed old mansion, with a bit of foliage showing over a high wall at one side. A bright plate embellished the door and bore the name Héger. A Latin inscription in the wall of the house showed it to have been given to the Guild of Royal Archers by the Infanta Isabelle early in the seventeenth century. Long before that the garden had been the orchard and herbary of a convent and the Hospital for the Poor.

We were detained at the door long enough to remember Lucy standing there, trembling and anxious, awaiting admission, and then we too were " let in by a *bonne* in a smart cap," apparently a fit successor to the Rosine of other days, and entered the corridor. This was paved with blocks of black and white marble and had painted walls. It extended through the entire depth of the house, and at its farther extremity an open door afforded us a glimpse of the garden. We were ushered into the little *salon* at the left of the passage, the one often mentioned in " Villette," and here we made known our wish to see the garden and class-rooms, and met with a prompt refusal from the neat portress. We tried diplomacy (also lucre) without avail: it was the *grandes vacances,* M. Héger was engaged, we could not be gratified,—unless, indeed, we were patrons of the school. At this juncture a portly, ruddy-faced lady of middle age and most courteous of speech and manner appeared, and, addressing us in faultless English, introduced herself as Mdlle. Héger, co-directress of the school, and " wholly at our service." In response to our apologies for the intrusion and explanations of the desire which had prompted it, we received complaisant assurances of welcome; yet the manner of our entertainer indicated that she did not share in our admiration and enthusiasm for Charlotte Brontë and her books. In the subsequent conversation it appeared that Mademoiselle and her family hold decided opinions upon the subject,—something more than mere lack of admiration. She was familiar with the novels, and thought that, while they exhibit a talent certainly not above mediocrity, they reflect the injustice, the untruthfulness, and the ingratitude of their creator. We were obliged to confess to ourselves that the family have reason for this view, when we reflected that in the books Miss Brontë has assailed their religion and disparaged the school and the characters of the teachers and pupils, has depicted Madame Héger in the odious duad of Madame Beck and Mdlle. Reuter, has represented M. Héger as the scheming and deceitful Pelet and the preposterous Paul, Lucy Snowe's lover; that this lover was the husband of Madame Héger, and father of the family of children to whom Lucy was at first *bonne d'enfants*, and that possibly the daughter she has described as the thieving, vicious Désirée—"that tadpole Désirée Beck" —was this very lady now so politely entertaining

us. To all this add the significant fact that
"Villette" is an autobiographical novel, which
"records the most vivid passages in Miss
Brontë's own sad heart's history," not a few of
the incidents being transcripts "from the darkest
chapter of her own life," and the light which
the consideration of this fact throws upon her
relations with members of the family will help
us to apprehend the stand-point from which the
Hégers judge Miss Brontë and her work, and to
excuse a natural resentment against one who has
presented them in a decidedly bad light. How
bad we realized when, during the ensuing chat,
we called to mind just what she had written of
them. As Madame Beck, Madame Héger had
been represented as lying, deceitful, and shame-
less, as "watching and spying everywhere,
peeping through every key-hole, listening behind
every door," as duplicating Lucy's keys and
secretly searching her bureau, as meanly ab-
stracting her letters and reading them to others,
as immodestly laying herself out to entrap the
man to whom she had given her love unsought.
It was some accession to the existing animosity
between herself and Madame Héger which pre-
cipitated Miss Brontë's departure from the *pensionnat*. Mrs. Gaskell ascribes their mutual dislike to Charlotte's free expression of her aversion
to the Catholic Church, of which Madame

The Hégers

Héger was a devotee, and hence "wounded in her most cherished opinions;" but a later writer plainly intimates that Miss Brontë hated the woman who sat for Madame Beck because marriage had given to *her* the man whom Miss Brontë loved, and that "Madame Beck had need to be a detective in her own house." The death of Madame Héger had rendered the family, who held her only as a sacred memory, more keenly sensitive than ever to anything which would seem by implication to disparage her.

For himself, it would appear that M. Héger had less cause for resentment; for, although in "Villette" his double is pictured as "a waspish little despot," as detestably ugly, in his anger closely resembling "a black and sallow tiger," as having an "overmastering love of authority and public display," as playing the spy and reading purloined letters, and in the Brontë epistles Charlotte declares he is choleric and irritable, compels her to make her French translations without a dictionary or grammar, and then has "his eyes almost plucked out of his head" by the occasional English word she is obliged to introduce, etc., yet all this is partially atoned for by the warm praise she subsequently accords him for his goodness to her and his disinterested friendship, by the poignant regret she

expresses at parting with him,—perhaps wholly
expiated by the high compliment she pays him
of making her heroine fall in love with him, or
the higher compliment it is suspected she paid
him of falling in love with him herself. One
who reads the strange history of passion in
" Villette," in conjunction with her letters,
" will know more of the truth of her stay in
Brussels than if a dozen biographers had undertaken to tell the whole tale." Still, M. Héger
can hardly be pleased by having members of his
school set forth as stupid, animal, and inferior,
" their principles rotten to the core, steeped in
systematic sensuality," by having his religion
styled " besotted papistry, a piece of childish
humbug," and the like. Something of the dis-
pleasure of the family was revealed in the course
of our conversation with Mdlle. Héger, but the
specific causes were but cursorily touched upon.
She could have no personal recollection of the
Brontës; her knowledge of them was derived
from her parents and the teachers,—presumably
the " repulsive old maids" of Charlotte's letters.
One teacher whom we saw in the school had
been a classmate of Charlotte's here. The
Brontës had not been popular with the school.
Their " heretical" religion had something to do
with this; but their manifest avoidance of the
other pupils during hours of recreation, Mad-

emoiselle thought, had been a more potent cause,
—Emily, in particular, not speaking with her
school-mates or teachers, except when obliged to
do so. The other pupils thought them of out-
landish accent and manners, and ridiculously old
to be at school at all,—being twenty-four and
twenty-six, and seeming even older. Their
sombre and ugly costumes were fruitful causes
of mirth to the gay young Belgian misses. The
Brontës were not brilliant students, and none of
their companions had ever suspected that they
were geniuses. Of the two, Emily was considered to be the more talented, but she was obsti-
nate and opinionated. Some of the pupils had
been inclined to resist having Charlotte placed
over them as teacher, and may have been muti-
nous. After her return from Haworth she
taught English to M. Héger and his brother-in-
law. M. Héger gave the sisters private lessons
in French without charge, and for some time
preserved their compositions, which Mrs. Gaskell copied. Mrs. Gaskell visited the *pensionnat*
in quest of material for her biography of Charlotte, and received all the aid M. Héger could
afford: the information thus obtained was, we
were told, fairly used. Miss Brontë's letters
from Brussels, so freely quoted in Mrs. Gaskell's
"Life," were addressed to Ellen Nussy, a familiar friend of Charlotte's, whose signature we saw

in the register at Haworth as witness to Miss
Brontë's marriage. The Hégers had no suspicion that she had been so unhappy with them
as these letters indicate, and she had assigned a
totally different reason for her sudden return to
England. She had been introduced to Madame
Héger by Mrs. Jenkins, wife of the then chap-
lain of the British Embassy at the Court of Belgium ; she had frequently visited that lady and
other friends in Brussels,—among them Mary
and Martha Taylor and the family of a Dr. ——
(*not* " Dr. John"),—and therefore her life here
need not have been so lonely and desolate as it
was made to appear.

The Hégers usually have a few English pupils
in the school, but have never had an American.
American tourists have before called to look at
the garden, but the family are not pleased by
the notoriety with which Miss Brontë has invested it. However, Mdlle. Héger kindly offered
to conduct us over any portion of the establishment we might care to see, and led the way along
the corridor to the narrow, high-walled garden.
We found it smaller than in the time when Miss
Brontë loitered here in weariness and solitude.
Mdlle. Héger explained that, while the width
remained the same, the erection of class-rooms
for the day-pupils had diminished the length by
some yards. Tall houses surrounded and shut

it in on either side, making it close and sombre, and the noises of the great city all about it penetrated only as a far-away murmur. There was a plat of verdant turf in the centre, bordered by scant flowers and gravelled walks, along which shrubs of evergreen were irregularly disposed. A few seats were here and there within the shade, where, as in Miss Brontë's time, the *externats* ate the lunch brought with them to the school; and overlooking it all stood the great pear-trees, whose gnarled and deformed trunks were relics of the time of the convent. Beyond these and along the gray wall which bounded the farther side of the enclosure was the sheltered walk which was Miss Brontë's favorite retreat, the *"allée défendue"* of her novels. It was screened by shrubs and perfumed by flowers, and, being secure from the intrusion of pupils, we could well believe that Charlotte and her heroine found here restful seclusion. The coolness and quiet and, more than all, the throng of vivid associations which filled the place tempted us to linger. The garden was not a spacious nor even a pretty one, and yet it seemed to us singularly pleasing and familiar, as if we were revisiting it after an absence. Seated upon a rustic bench close at hand, possibly the very one which Lucy had "reclaimed from fungi and mould," how the memories came surging up in our minds! How often in the summer twilight poor Charlotte had lingered here in solitude after the day's burdens and trials with " stupid and impertinent" pupils ! How often, with weary feet and a dreary heart, she had paced this secluded walk and thought, with longing, of the dear ones in far-away Haworth parsonage ! In this sheltered corner her other self, Lucy, sat and listened to the distant chimes and thought forbidden thoughts and cherished impossible hopes. Here she met and talked with Dr. John. Deep beneath this " Methuselah of a pear-tree," the one nearest the end of the alley, lies the imprisoned dust of the poor nun who was buried alive ages ago for some sin against her vow, and whose perambulating ghost so disquieted poor Lucy. At the root of this same tree one miserable night Lucy buried her precious letters, and meant also to bury a grief and her great affection for Dr. John. Here she leant her brow against Methuselah's knotty trunk and uttered to herself those brave words of renunciation, " Good-night, Dr. John ; you are good, you are beautiful, *but you are not mine. Good-night, and God bless you !"* Here she held pleasant converse with M. Paul, and with him, spellbound, saw the ghost of the nun descend from the leafy shadows overhead and, sweeping close past their wondering faces, disappear behind yonder screen of shrubbery into the darkness of the summer night. By that tall tree next the class-rooms the ghost was wont to ascend to meet its material sweetheart, Fanshawe, in the great garret beneath yonder skylight,—the garret where Lucy retired to read Dr. John's letter, and wherein M. Paul confined her to learn her part in the vaudeville for Madame Beck's *fête*-day. In this nook where we sat " The Professor" had walked and talked with and almost made love to Mdlle. Reuter, and from yonder window overlooking the alley had seen that perfidious fair one in dalliance with Pelet beneath these pear-trees. From that window M. Paul watched Lucy as she sat or walked in the *allée défendue*, dogged by Madame Beck ; from the same window were thrown the love-letters which fell at Lucy's feet sitting here. Leaves from the overhanging boughs were plucked for us as souvenirs of the place ; then, reverently traversing once more the narrow alley so often traced in weariness by Charlotte Brontë, we turned away. From the garden we entered the long and spacious class-room of the first and second divisions. A movable partition divided it across the middle when the classes were in session ; the floor was of bare boards cleanly scoured. There were long ranges of desks and benches upon either side, and a lane through the middle led up to a raised platform at the end

of the room, where the instructor's chair and
desk were placed.

How quickly our fancy peopled the place!
On these front seats sat the gay and indocile
Belgian girls. There, "in the last row, in the
quietest corner, sat Emily and Charlotte side by
side, insensible to anything about them;" and
at the same desk, "in the farthest seat of the
farthest row," sat Mdlle. Henri during Crimsworth's English lessons. Here Lucy's desk was
rummaged by Paul and the tell-tale odor of
cigars left behind. Here, after school-hours,
Miss Brontë taught Héger English, he taught
her French, and Paul taught Lucy arithmetic
and (incidentally) love. This was the scene of
their *tête-à-têtes*, of his efforts to persuade her
into his religious faith, of their ludicrous supper of biscuit and baked apples, and of his final
violent outbreak with Madame Beck, when she
literally thrust herself between him and his love.
From this platform Crimsworth and Lucy and
Charlotte Brontë herself had given instruction
to pupils whose insubordination had first to be
confronted and overcome. Here Paul and Héger
gave lectures upon literature, and Paul delivered
his spiteful tirade against the English on the
morning of his *fête*-day. Upon this desk were
heaped his bouquets that morning; from its
smooth surface poor Lucy dislodged and fract-

ured his spectacles; and here, seated in Paul's chair, at Paul's desk, we saw and were presented to Paul Emanuel himself,—M. Héger.

It was something more than curiosity which made us alert to note the appearance and manner of this man, who has been so nearly associated with Miss Brontë in an intercourse which colored her subsequent life and determined her life-work, who has been made the hero of her novels and has been deemed the hero of her own heart's romance; and yet we *were* curious to know what manner of man it was who has been so much as suspected of being honored with the love and preference of the dainty Charlotte Brontë. During a short conversation with him we had opportunity to observe that in person this "wise, good, and religious" man must, at the time Miss Brontë knew him, have more closely resembled Pelet of "The Professor" than any other of her pen-portraits: indeed, after the lapse of more than forty years that delineation still, for the most part, aptly applied to him. He was of middle size, of rather spare habit of body; his face was fair and the features pleasing and regular, the cheeks were thin and the mouth flexible, the eyes—somewhat sunken—were mild blue and of singularly pleasant expression. We found him aged and somewhat infirm; his finely-shaped head was fringed with white hair, and partial baldness contributed reverence to his presence and tended to enhance the intellectual effect of his wide brow. In repose his countenance showed a hint of melancholy: as Miss Brontë said, his "physiognomy was *fine et spirituelle;*" one would hardly imagine it could ever resemble the "visage of a black and sallow tiger." His voice was low and soft, his bow still "very polite, not theatrical, scarcely French," his manner *suave* and courteous, his dress scrupulously neat. He accosted us in the language Miss Brontë taught him forty years ago, and his accent and diction honored her instruction. He was talking with some patrons, and, as his daughter had hinted that he was averse to speaking of Miss Brontë, we soon took leave of him and were shown other parts of the school. The other class-rooms, used for less advanced pupils, were smaller. In one of them Miss Brontë had ruled as monitress after her return from Haworth. The large dormitory of the *pensionnat* was above the long class-room, and in the time of the Brontës most of the boarders—about twenty in number—slept here. Their cots were arranged along either side, and the position of those occupied by the Brontës was pointed out to us at the extreme end of the room. It was here that Lucy suffered the horrors of hypochondria, so graphically portrayed in "Villette," and found the discarded costume of the spectral nun lying upon her bed, and here Miss Brontë passed those nights of wakeful misery which Mrs. Gaskell describes. A long, narrow room in front of the class-rooms was shown us as the *réfectoire*, where the Brontës, with the other boarders, took their meals, presided over by M. and Madame Héger, and where, during the evenings, the lessons for the ensuing days were prepared. Here were held the evening prayers which Charlotte used to avoid by escaping into the garden. This, too, was the scene of Paul's readings to teachers and pupils, and of some of his spasms of petulance, which readers of "Villette" will remember. From the *réfectoire* we passed again into the corridor, where we made our adieus to our affable conductress. She explained that, whereas this establishment had been both a *pensionnat* and an *externat*, having about seventy day-pupils and twenty boarders when Miss Brontë was here, it was after the death of Madame Héger used as a day-school only,—the *pensionnat* being in another street.

The genuine local color Miss Brontë gives in "Villette" enabled us to be sure that we had found the sombre old church where Lucy, arrested in passing by the sound of the bells, knelt upon the stone pavement, passing thence

into the confessional of Père Silas. Certain it
is that this old church lies upon the route she
would take in the walk from the school to the
Protestant cemetery, which she had set out to
do that afternoon, and the narrow streets which
lie beyond the church correspond to those in
which she was lost. Certain, too, it is said to
be that this incident is taken from her own experience. Reid says, " During one of the long
holidays, when her mind was restless and disturbed, she found sympathy, if not peace, in the
counsels of a priest in the confessional, who
soothed her troubled spirit without attempting
to enmesh it in the folds of Romanism."

Our way to the Protestant cemetery—a spot
sadly familiar to Miss Brontë, and the usual
termination of her walks—lay past the site of
the Porte de Louvain and out to the hills beyond the old city limits. From our path we
saw more than one tree-shrouded farm-house
which might have been the place of Paul's
breakfast with his school, and at least one quaint
mansion, with green-tufted and terraced lawns,
which might have served Miss Brontë as the
model for La Terrasse, the suburban home of the
Brettons and the temporary abode of the Taylor
sisters whom she visited here. From the cemetery we beheld vistas of farther lines of hills,
of intervening valleys, of farms and villas, and

of the great city lying below.   Miss Brontë has well described this place : " Here, on pages of stone and of brass, are written names, dates, last tributes of pomp or love, in English, French, German, and Latin."   There are stone crosses all about, and great thickets of roses and yews ; " cypresses that stand straight and mute, and willows that hang low and still ;" and there are " dim garlands of everlasting flowers."   Here " The Professor" found his long-sought sweetheart kneeling at a new-made grave under the overhanging trees.   And here *we* found the shrine of poor Charlotte Brontë's many pilgrimages hither,—the burial-place of her friend and school-mate, the Jessy Yorke of " Shirley ;" the spot where, under " green sod and a gray marble head-stone, cold, coffined, solitary, Jessy sleeps below."

LEMAN'S SHRINES

Beloved of Littérateurs—Gibbon—D'Aubigné—Rousseau—Byron—Shelley—Dickens, etc.—Scenes of Childe Harold—Nouvelle Heloïse—Prisoner of Chillon—Land of Byron.

A PILGRIMAGE in the track of Childe Harold brings us from the shores of Albion, by Belgium's capital and deadly Waterloo, along the castled Rhine and over mountain-pass to " Italia, home and grave of empires," and to the sublimer scenery of " Manfred," " Chillon," and the third canto of the pilgrim-poet's master-piece; to his " silver-sheeted Staubbach" and "arrowy Rhone," "soaring Jungfrau" and "bleak Mont Blanc." We linger with especial pleasure on the shores of " placid Leman," in an enchanting region which teems with literary shrines and is pervaded with memories and associations—often so thrilling and vivid that they seem like veritable and sensible presences —of the brilliant number who have here had their haunts. Here Calvin wrought his Commentaries; here Voltaire polished his darts; here Rousseau laid the scenes of his impassioned tale; here Dickens, Byron, and Shelley loitered and wrote; here Gibbon and de Staël, Schlegel and Constant, and many another scarcely less famous, lived and wrought the treasures of their knowledge and fancy into the literature of the

226

Haunts of Littérateurs

world. A lingering voyage round the lake, like
that of Byron and Shelley, is a delight to be remembered through a lifetime, and affords opportunity to visit the spots consecrated by genius upon
these shores. At Geneva we find the inn where
Byron lodged and first met the author of " Queen
Mab," the house in which Rousseau was born,
the place where d'Aubigné wrote his history,
the sometime home of John Calvin. Near by,
in a house presented by the Genevese after his
release from the long imprisonment suffered on
their account, dwelt Bonnivard, Byron's immortal " Prisoner of Chillon," and here he suffered
from his procession of wives and finally died.
Just beyond the site of the fortifications, on the
east side of the city, is an eminence whose slopes
are tastefully laid out with walks that wind,
amid sward and shrub, to the observatory which
crowns the summit and marks the site of Bonnivard's Priory of St. Victor, lost to him by his
devotion to Genevan independence. Not far
away is the public library, founded by his be-
quest of his modest collection of books and MSS.
which we see here carefully preserved. Here
also is an old portrait of the prisoner, which
represents him as a reckless and jolly " good
fellow" rather than a saintly hero, and accords
better with his character as described by late
writers than with the common conception of him.

A Literary Pilgrimage

Byron loved this Leman lake, and it is said his discontented sprite still walks its margins; certain it is he remains its poetic genius; his melody seems to wake in every breeze that stirs its surface. The Villa Diodati, a plain, quadrangular, three-storied mansion of moderate dimensions, standing on the shore a few miles from Geneva, was the handsome "Giaour's" first home after his separation from Lady Byron and his exile from England. It had been the residence of the Genevan Professor Diodati and the sojourn of his friend the poet Milton. Pleasant vineyards surround the place and slope away to the water, but there is little in the spot or its near environment to commend it to the fancy of a poet. Byron's study here was a sombre room at the back from which neither the lake nor the snowy peaks were visible, and here he wrote, besides many minor poems, " Manfred," " Prometheus," " Darkness," " Dream," and the third canto of " Childe Harold." Here also he wrote " Marriage of Belphegor," a tale setting forth his version of his own infelicitous marriage; but hearing that his wife was seriously ill, he burned it in his study fire. From here, by instigation of de Staël, he sent to Lady Byron ineffectual overtures for a reconciliation. His companion at the villa was an eccentric Italian physician, Polidori, who was uncle to the poet

Byron at Villa Diodati—Shelley

Rossetti, and who here quarrelled with Byron's guests and wrote " The Vampire," a weird production afterward attributed to Byron. Lovers of Byron owe much to his sojourn on Leman; he found in the inspiring landscapes here, especially in the environment of mountains, a power that profoundly stirred what his wife called " the angel in him." His letters recognize an afflatus breathed upon him by the " majesty around and above," and the quality of the poems here produced shows his yielding and response to that benign influence; many a gem of poetic thought was here begotten of lake and mount and cataract, which otherwise had never been. The insincere stanzas of some of his later poems would scarcely have been written on Leman. As we muse in the spots he frequented—wandering on the entrancing margins or floating on the crystal waters—and look thence upon the snow-crowned peaks, resplendent in the sunshine or roseate in the after-glow, we aspire to not only partake of his rapture in this sublime beauty, but to appreciate the deeper feelings to which it moved him.

A villa near Byron's, and reached by a path through his grounds,—Maison Chapuis, of Mont Allegra,—was occupied that summer by the " impassioned Ariel of English verse," with Mary Shelley and her brunette relative Jane Clermont

(the Claire of Shelley's journal), who after bore
to Byron a daughter called Alba by the Shelleys,
but later named by Byron Allegra, for the
place where he had known the mother. At
Mont Allegra " Bridge of Arve," " Intellectual
Beauty," and Mrs. Shelley's weird " Franken-
stein" were penned. Here Byron was a daily visitant, and the Shelleys were the usual companions
of his excursions upon the lake of beauty, in a
picturesque lateen-rigged boat which was the
property of the poets and the counterpart of
which we see moored by the Diodati shore,
looking like a bit of the Levant transported to
this tramontane water. The " white phantom"
observed by telescopists on the opposite shore to
sometimes embark with Byron, and which he
gravely told Madame de Staël was his dog, was
doubtless the frail Claire. The admonitions of
de Staël anent his mode of life provoked Byron
to take sure revenge by being attentive to her
husband, which the overshadowing wife always
resented as an affront upon herself. It is said
the poet's observation of this pair prompted the
couplet of " Don Juan :"

> " But oh ! ye lords of ladies intellectual,
>   Inform us truly, have they not henpecked you all ?"

Passing for the present the shrines of Ferney
and Coppet, we find in picturesque Lausanne the

quaint house in which Voltaire lived several winters, and not far away the place where Secretan died a few months ago. Gibbon's dwelling has been demolished, but we find the place of his summer-house where the great history was completed, and of his famous rose-tree where Byron gathered roses long ago. Madame de Genlis narrates this incident of the great "Decliner and Faller" at Lausanne : he was enamoured of the comely Madame Crousaz, and, finding her alone, he knelt at her feet and besought her love. He received an unfavorable reply, but remained in his humble posture until the lady, after repeatedly requesting him to arise, discovered that his weight made it impossible, and summoned a servant to assist him to regain his feet. His obesity seems to have been a standing jest among his acquaintances : a sufferer from indigestion, due to lack of exercise, was advised by a witty friend to " walk twice around Gibbon before breakfast." Several decades later another illustrious English man of letters sojourned in Lausanne. A pretty cottage-villa, with embowered walls and flower-shaded porticos which look from a mild eminence across the crescentic lake, was, in 1846, the dwelling of Dickens, who here wrote one of the matchless Christmas stories and a part of " Dombey and Son." From the magnificent slope of Lausanne

A Literary Pilgrimage

the whole lake region is visible, with the dark Juras rising to the western horizon, the Alps of Savoy, and "the monarch of mountains with a diadem of snow" upholding the sky away in the south. At the foot of this slope is the port-town of Ouchy, a resort of Byron's in his sailing excursions ; at the plain little Anchor inn near the *quai* (Byron called it a "wretched inn") he lodged, and here, being detained two days (June 26 and 27, 1816) by a storm which overtook him on his return from Chillon and Clarens, he wrote the touching "Prisoner of Chillon." In a parsonage not far from Lausanne was reared sweet Suzanne Curchod, erst *fiancée* of Gibbon, and later the mother of de Staël.

Eastward is "Clarens, birthplace of deep love," whose "air is the breath of passionate thought, whose trees take root in love ;" about it lies the charming region which Rousseau chose for his fiction and peopled with affections, and where Byron, Houghton, and Shelley loved to linger. Here the latter first read "Nouvelle Héloïse" amid the settings of its scenes ; here Byron wrote many glowing lines, inspired by the beauty and romantic associations around him. From the vine-clad terraces which cling to the heights we behold the view which enraptured the poet,—a broad expanse of lacustrine beauty and Alpine sublimity, embracing the

Leman shores from the Rhone to the Juras of
Gex, the entire width of the *" bleu impossible"*
lake and Alp piled on Alp beyond.   Back of
Clarens we find the spot of Rousseau's " Bosquet
de Julie," and, at a little distance among embow-
ering trees, the birthplace of a woman stranger
than any fancied character of his fiction, the
Madame de Warens of his " Confessions."

Between Clarens and Villeneuve, on an
isolated rock whose base is laved by Leman's
waters, which " meet and flow a thousand feet
in depth below," stands the grim prison of
Chillon, the scene of Byron's poem.   The
fortress is an irregular pile of masonry, and,
with its massive walls, loop-holed towers, and
white battlements, is a picturesque object seen
across wide reaches of the lake.   The present
structure is a hoary successor to a stronghold
still more ancient : the prehistoric lake-dwellers
here had a fortress and were succeeded by the
Franks and Romans.   Of the present structure,
the Romanesque columns and the range of dungeons are known to have been in existence in
830, when Count Wala, a cousin of Charlemagne,
for alluding to the wife of Louis the Debonair
as " that adulterous woman," was incarcerated
here.   Thus Judith's reputation was vindicated
and the earliest certain date of this fortress fixed.
The present superstructure remains unchanged

since the thirteenth century. It is now connected with the shore by a wooden structure
which spans the moat and replaces the ancient
drawbridge. Through a massive gate-way we
enter a roughly-paved court, whence a bluff
Savoyard conducts us through the romantic pile.
Among the apartments of the ducal family we
see the banqueting-hall where the dukes held
roistering wassail; the kitchen on whose great
hearth oxen were roasted whole; the Chamber
of Inquisition where hapless prisoners were tortured to extort confession, this room being near
the chamber of the duchess, into which—despite its thick wall—the shrieks of the tortured
must have sometimes penetrated and disturbed
Her Serene Highness. Outside her door is a
post to which the wretches were bound, and it is
scored by marks of the irons which cauterized
their flesh; in a near corner stood a rack which
rent them limb from limb. The crypt beneath,
with its low arched vaults and its graceful pillars
rising out of the rock, is the most interesting
portion of the fortress. Referring to their
architectural perfection, Longfellow once said
these were the " most delightful dungeons he ever
saw," but as we stand in their twilight gloom
the horrors of their history weigh heavily on
the heart. During this century the castle has
been used as an arsenal, but occasionally also

Prison of Chillon

as a prison, and Byron found some of these
"chambers of sorrow" tenanted at the time
of his visits. One contracted cell is that in
which the condemned passed their last night of
life chained upon a rock, near the beam upon
which they were strangled and the opening
through which their bodies were thrust into the
lake. Another vault contains a pit or well, with
a spiral stair down which poor dupes stepped
into a yawning depth and—eternity. A third
chamber, so dark that its grotesque carvings are
scarcely discernible and no missal could be read
by daylight, was the chapel of the fortress.
Traversing the succession of dungeons, we .come
to the last and largest, and reverently stand
beside the column where Byron's prisoner was
chained. This "dungeon deep and old" lies
not beneath the level of the lake, as Byron
believed, yet it is sufficiently dank and dismal to
be the appropriate scene of the touching and
tragic story which he located here. It is a long,
crypt-like apartment, whose vaulted roof of rock
is upheld by the "seven pillars of Gothic
mould" aligned along the middle. It is dimly
lighted by loop-holes pierced in the ponderous
walls for the feudal bowmen ; through these
narrow apertures, where the prisoner "felt the
winter's spray wash through the bars when winds
were high," we look out, as did he, upon the

distant town, "the lake with its white sails," the "mountains high," and the little Isle de Paix —"scarce broader than the dungeon floor"— gleaming like an emerald from a setting of amethyst. Here is Bonnivard's chain, scarce four feet long, and in the central pillar the ring which held it. The light, falling aslant "through the cleft of the thick wall" upon the floor, shows us the pathway worn in the rock by the pacing of the prisoner during the weary years, and reveals—graven on the column-stone by the poet's hand—the name Byron.

At Chillon we are in the midst of a region pervaded by the sentiment of the pilgrim-poet. The Byron path leads from the shore to the broad terraces of the Hôtel Byron, whence we behold as in a picture the romantic scene his poetry portrays,—the "mountains with their thousand years of snow," the shimmering water of "the wide long lake," the dark slopes of the Juras terraced to their summits, the "white-walled towns" upon the nearer hill-sides. Directly before us—bearing its three tall trees —"the little isle, the only one in view," smiles in our faces from the bosom of the water; on the right we see sweet Clarens and the pictu-resque battlements of Chillon; on the left, the glittering peaks of Dent du Midi and the Alps of Savoy, with the "Rhone in fullest flow" between the rocky heights; while from the farther shore rise the cliffs of Meillerie, at whose base Byron and Shelley, clinging to their frail boat, narrowly escaped a watery grave on the very spot where St. Preux and Julia of "Nouvelle Héloïse" were rescued from the same fate.

Our farewell view of this Land of Byron is taken on a cloudless summer night, when the radiance of the harvest moon exalts and glorifies all the scene; the grim prison of Bonnivard is transformed into a snowy palace of peaceful delights, the white mountain-peaks gleam with the chaste lustre of pearls, the vine-embowered village on the shore seems an Aidenn of purity and light, and the sheen of the tremulous water is that of a sea of molten silver. Surely, on all her round, "Luna lights no spot more fair."

CHÂTEAUX OF FERNEY AND COPPET

Voltaire's Home, Church, Study, Garden, Relics–Literary Court of de Staël–Mementos–Famous Rooms, Guests–Schlegel–Shelley–Constant–Byron–Davy, etc.–De Staël's Tomb.

A LITERARY pilgrimage on Leman's shores that did not include Ferney among its shrines would be obviously incomplete. No matter how widely we may dissent from his opinions or how much we may deplore some of his utterances, the brilliant philosopher who for so many years inhabited that spot and made it the intellectual capital of the world commands a place in letters which we may neither gainsay nor ignore, and the Château Voltaire is to many visitors one of the chief objects of interest in the neighborhood of Geneva.

Beneath a summer sky a delightful jaunt of a few miles, among orchards and vineyards and past the ancestral home of Albert Gallatin, brings us to Voltaire's domain in Gex. The mansion and town of Ferney were alike the creation of the *genius loci ;* he was architect and builder of both. The town and its factories were erected to give shelter and employment to hundreds of artisans who appealed to him against oppressive employers at Geneva. The place has obviously degenerated since his time; an air of shabbiness and thriftlessness prevails, and ancient smells by no means suggestive of "the odors of Araby the blest" obtrude upon the pilgrim. At the public fountain stout-armed women were washing family linen manifestly long unused to such manipulation. Near by dwell descendants of Voltaire's secretary Wagnière. Upon a verdant plateau farther away, in the heart of one of the most beautiful regions of earth, "girdled by eighty leagues of mountains that pierce the sky," was Voltaire's last home. By its gate is the little church he built, bearing upon its gable his inscription "Deo Erexit Voltaire." Here he attended mass with his niece, and, as *seigneur*, was always incensed by the priest; here he gave in marriage his adopted daughters; here he preached a homily against theft; and here he built for himself a tomb, projecting into the side of the church,— "neither within nor without," as he explained to a guest,—where he hoped to be buried. The church was long used as a tenement, later it has been a storage- and tool-house. The château is a spacious and dignified three-storied structure of Italian style, attractive in appearance and well suited to one of Voltaire's tastes and occupations. The exterior has been somewhat

altered, but the apartments of the philosopher
are essentially unchanged. The late proprietor
preserved the study and bedroom nearly as Voltaire left them when he started upon his fatal
visit to Paris. They are small, with high
ceilings, quaint carvings, faded tapestries, and
are obviously planned to facilitate the work of
the busiest author the world has known, who
here, after the age of threescore, wrote a
hundred and sixty works. Many of these assailed the church authorities, who had shown
themselves capable of punishing mere difference
of opinion by the rack and the stake, but "the
religion of the Sermon on the Mount and the
character of men of good and consistent lives"
they did not attack: some of the books were
cursed at Rome, some at Geneva, others were
burned at both places.

Disposed in Voltaire's rooms we have seen his
heavy furniture; his study-chair standing by the
table upon which he wrote half of each day;
his beautiful porcelain stove, a gift from Fred-
erick the Great; a draped mausoleum bearing
an inscription by Voltaire and designed by his
protégé to contain his heart; many paintings
presented by royal admirers,—Albani's "Toilet
of Venus," Titian's "Venus and Love," a picture
of Voltaire's chimney-sweep, portrait of Lekain
who acted so many of Voltaire's tragedies, por-

traits of that philosopher, a fanciful deification of him by Duplessis; on the same wall, coarse engravings of Washington and Franklin. Franklin was the firm friend of Voltaire, and it was his letters which first brought to Ferney news of the Declaration of Independence. The discolored embroidery of Voltaire's bed and armchair was wrought by his niece Madame Denis, "the little fat woman round as a ball." Habitually complaining of illness in his last years, he spent more than half his time in this quaint bed. He had a desk, containing writing materials, suspended above the bed so that he could write here day or night, and the amount of work he thus accomplished is astounding : in the last four years of feeble life he wrote thirty works varying in size from a pamphlet to a ponderous tome. His breakfast was served in bed, and here he habitually attended to his correspondence, which included most of the sovereigns of Europe and the learned and great of all climes. In this bed he once lay for weeks feigning mortal illness, and thus induced the priest to give him the *viaticum.* This bedroom, too, was the scene of many quarrels with his niece regarding her extravagances, but as we sit in his chair by his bedside we prefer to recall more pleasing incidents the room has witnessed ; here he dictated to Marie Corneille the ardent words which brought reparation to many a cruelly wronged family; this was the scene of his many pleasantries with the house-keeper "Baba," and of the loving ministrations of his sweet ward "Belle et Bonne."

Many of Voltaire's belongings have been removed and his estate has been shorn of its vast dimensions, but much remains to remind us of the genius of the place. Here are the gardens, lawns, and shrubberies he planted; on this turf-grown terrace beneath his study windows he paced as he planned his compositions, and here, at the age of eighty-three, he evolved "Irene" and parts of "Agathocles;" near by are his fount, his arbored promenade, the shaded spot where he wrote in summer days, the place of the lightning-rod made for him by Franklin. Long reaches of the hedge were rooted by him, many of the trees are from the nursery he cultured, the cedars were raised from seeds sent to him by the Empress Catherine. A venerable tree in the park was planted by Voltaire's own hands: when we point to a blemish upon its trunk and ask our guide, whose family have dwelt on the estate since the time of Voltaire, if that is the effect of lightning, as has been averred, he indignantly declares the only damage the tree ever sustained has been from visitors who, to secure souvenirs of the illustrious phi-

losopher, would destroy the whole tree were he
not alert to protect it.

For twenty years this home of Voltaire was
the centre and pharos of the intellectual world.
To this court kings sent couriers with proffers of
honors and assurances of esteem; hither came
legions of *littérateurs*, academicians, politicians,
eager to hail the savant or to secure his commen-
dation. "All roads then led to Ferney as they
once did to Rome," and the hospitalities of the
château were so taxed that Voltaire declared he
was innkeeper for all Europe. He habitually
complained of the climate here, "Lapland in
winter, Naples in summer;" during some seasons
"thirty leagues of snow were visible from his
windows;" but on the July day of our visit the
atmosphere is exquisitely delightful and Voltaire's
"desert" seems a paradise. Behind us rise the
vine-clad slopes of Jura, below lies the lake like
an amethystine sea, afar gleam the snow-crowned
peaks, and about us in the old gardens are the
golden sunshine, the incense of flowers, the
twitter of birds, and all the charm of sweet
summer-time. As we linger in the spots he loved
it is pleasant to recall the good that mingled in
the oddly composite nature of the daring old
man who inhabited this beautiful scene and
created much of its beauty; to remember that
dumb creatures loved him and fed from his hand;

that the destitute and oppressed never vainly applied to him for succor or protection; that in varying phrase he solemnly averred, in letters of counsel to youthful admirers in his own and other lands, " We are in the world only for the good we can do."

Of the galaxy of *littérateurs* who had home or haunt by Leman's margins Madame de Staël, by her long residence and many incidents of her career, seems most closely associated with this region of delights. The château of Coppet has for two centuries belonged to her family; here some portion of her girlhood was passed; here she found asylum from the horrors of the French Revolution and residence when Napoleon banished her from his capital. Later her son Auguste dwelt here, and the place is now the property of her great-granddaughter. Literary and social associations render this mediæval château one of the most interesting spots on earth. Exiled from the society of Paris, de Staël erected here a court which became the centre of intellectual Europe. Coppet was in itself a lustrous microcosm whose attraction was the conversation of its hostess and queen, which allured the wit and wisdom of a continent, making this court not only a literary centre, but a political power of which Napoleon, by his proscriptions, proclaimed his fear. The great number of illustrious courtiers who came to Coppet caused the priestess of its hospitalities to aver she needed "a cook whose heels were winged."

The darkly-verdured terraces of Jura on the one hand, the blue waters and the farther snowy peaks on the other, fitly environ the enchanting scene in the midst of which was set the abode of the greatest woman of her time. From Geneva a charming sail along the lake conveys us to her home and sepulchre. We approach the château between rows of venerable trees beneath which de Staël loitered with her guests. The stately edifice rises from three sides of a court, whence we are admitted to a large hall on the lower floor which she used as a theatre. These walls, which give back only the echo of our foot-falls, have resounded with the applause of fastidious auditors when the queen of Coppet, with her children and Récamier, de Sabran, Werner, Jenner, Constant, Von Vought, or Ida Brun acted upon a stage at yonder end of the room. The composition of plays for this theatre was sometime de Staël's principal recreation : these have been published as " Essais Dramatiques." But more ambitious dramas were presented ; the matchless Juliette acted here with Sabran and de Staël in " Semiramis ;" Werner assisted in the first presentation of " Attila," which was written here; Constant's " Wallenstein" was composed here and first produced on this stage, as was also Oehlenschläger's " Hakon Jarl." De Staël was an efficient actress, her lustrous eyes, superb arms, and strong and flexible voice compensating for deficiencies of training. A broad stair leads from the silent theatre to the principal apartments, among which we find the library where Necker wrote his " Politics and Finance," the grand salon and reception-rooms,—all of imposing dimensions and having parquetted floors. Arranged in these rooms are many mementos of the daughter of genius who once inhabited them,—hangings of tapestry ; antique spindle-legged furniture carved and gilded in quaint fashion ; the cherub-bedecked clock that stood above her desk ; her books and inkstand ; the desk upon which " Necker," " Ten Years of Exile," " Allemagne," and many minor treatises were written. Upon the wall is her portrait, by David, which pictures her with bare arms and shoulders, her head crowned by a nimbus of yellow turban which she wore when costumed as " Corinne :" the features are not classical, but the brunette face, with its splendid dark eyes, is comely as well as intellectual, and obviously contradicts Byron's declaration, " She is so ugly I wonder how the best intellect of France could have taken up such a residence." Schäffer's portrait of her daughter hangs near by, displaying a face of striking beauty, and a picture of Madame Necker, de Staël's mother, represents a sweet-faced woman who smiles upon the visitor despite the discomfort of a painfully tight-fitting dress of white satin. Here also are portraits of Necker, of de Staël's first husband, of her son Auguste, of Schlegel, and of other literary *confrères,* a statue of her father, by Tieck, and a bust of Rocca, her youthful second husband. The latter represents a finely-shaped head and a winning face. Byron thought Rocca notably handsome, and Frederica Brun testified, " he had the most magnificent head I ever saw." He was so slender that one of de Staël's courtiers wondered "how his many wounds found a place upon him :" these wounds, received in the Peninsula, won for him the sympathy of de Staël, which deepened into love.

As we wander through the rooms, waking the echoes and viewing the souvenirs of the illustrious dead, as we ponder their lives, their aims, their works, it seems, amid the vivid associations of the place, to require no supernal effort of the fancy to repeople it with the brilliant company who were wont to assemble here. Of these apartments, the salon, from whose wall looks down the portrait of Corinna, will longest hold the pilgrim. It was the throne-room of this court: here resorted a throng of the best and noblest minds, *littérateurs*, scientists, men of largest thought, of highest rank. Here Récamier was a frequent guest: yonder mirror, with its multipanes framed in gilt metal, often reflected her lovely face. In this room she danced for the delight of de Staël her famous gavotte, which had transported the *beau monde* of Paris, and was rewarded by its celebration in " Corinne." Some who came to this court remained as residential guests: for fifteen years Sismondi worked here upon his " Literature of Southern Europe," etc.; here the sage Bonstetten wrote many of his twenty-five volumes; here Schlegel, the great critic of his age, who is commemorated in " Corinne" as Castel-Forte, was installed for twelve years and prepared his works on dramatic literature; here Werner, author of " Luther," " Wanda," etc., wrote much of his mystic poetry; here the Danish national poet composed his noblest tragedies, " Correggio" being a souvenir of Coppet; here Constant penned many dramas. Among the frequenters of this salon were Madame de Saussure, famous for her books on education; Frederica Brun, with her daughter Ida who is imaged in " Allemagne;" Sir Humphry and Lady Davy, the latter being the realization of " Corinne;" Madame de Krüde-

ner, author of " Valérie," from whom Delphine
was mainly drawn ; Barante the critic ; Dumont,
editor of Jeremy Bentham.   Of those who
came less often were Cuvier, Gibbon, Ritter,
Lacretelle, Mirabeau, Houghton, Brougham,
Ampère, Byron, Shelley, Montmorency, Wy-
nona, Tieck, Müller, Candolle, de Sergey, Prince
Augustus, and scores of others.

This room, where that galaxy assembled, has
witnessed the most wonderful intellectual *séances*
of the century.   We may imagine something
of the brilliancy of an assembly of such minds
presided over by de Staël,—what gayety, what
coruscations of wit, what displays of wisdom,
what keenness of discussion were not possible to
such a circle!   For some time religious tenets
were frequently under consideration.   Every
shade of belief, doubt, and agnosticism had its
defenders in the company.   Sismondi was cor-
responding with Channing of Boston, whose
views he espoused, and the arrival of each letter
caused the renewal of the argument in which
de Staël was the principal advocate of the
spiritual motive of Christianity as against a
system of mere well-doing.   All questions of
literature, art, ethics, philosophy, politics, were
considered here by the most capable minds of
the age, the discussions being oft prolonged into
the night.   But that there may be too much

even of a good thing is naïvely confessed by
Bonstetten, one of the lights of these *séances*, in
his letters : " I feel tired by surfeit of intellect:
there is more mind expended at Coppet in a
day than in many countries in a year, but I am
half dead." Scintillant converse was inter-
spersed with music from the old harpsichord in
yonder corner,—touched by fingers that now are
dust,—with recitations and reading of MSS. It
was the habit of de Staël to read to the circle,
for their criticism, what she had written during
the morning, and to discuss the subsequent
chapters. Guests who were writing at the
château then read their compositions—Bonstetten's " Latium" often put the company to sleep—
and eagerly sought de Staël's suggestions ; " the
lesser lights were glad to borrow warmth and
lustre from the central sun." Châteauvieux
declares, " She formed my mental character ;
for twenty years my sentiments were founded
upon hers." Sismondi says, " She determined
my literary career ; her good sense guided my
pen." Bonstetten, Schlegel, Werner, and others
bear similar testimony to the value of her
counsel.

The place was never more animated than in
the last summer of her life, when Byron and
Shelley used to cross the lake to join the circle
in this room. De Staël had met Byron in Lon-

don during the ephemeral " Byron-madness," and now, in his social exile, her doors were freely open to him : his letters testify " she made Coppet as agreeable as society and talent can make any place on earth." Here he first saw " Glenarvon," a venomous attack upon him which seems to have served no purpose save to illustrate the aphorism about " a woman scorned," its authoress having been notoriously importunate for Byron's favor, even attempting, it was said, to enter his apartments in male attire. In this salon Mrs. Hervey, the novelist, feigned to faint at Byron's approach : from the balcony outside these windows, where de Staël and her father stood and saw Napoleon's army cross the Swiss frontier, Byron looked upon the scene which inspired some of his divinest stanzas. The château was a busy place in those years : a guest writes from here, " In every corner one is at a literary task ; de Staël is writing ' Exile,' Auguste and Constant a tragedy, Sabran an opera, Sismondi his ' Republics,' Bonstetten a philosophy, and Rocca his ' Spanish War.' "

One noble chamber hung with dim tapestries is that erst occupied by Récamier : it had before been the sick-room of Madame Necker and the scene of her husband's loving care of her, which de Staël so touchingly records. The chamber of de Staël is near by, its windows overlooking her sepulchre : here she wrote the books which made her fame ; here she instructed her children, their Sabbath lessons being from the devout treatises of her father and à Kempis's " Imitation of Christ," the book she read in her own dying hours. A smaller room, looking out upon the park, the terraces of Jura, and the white walls of Lausanne, was shared by Constant and Bonstetten. In the tower above have been found letters written by Gibbon to his *fiancée*, who became the mother of de Staël : they have been published by the grandson of de Staël, and show that the conduct of the great " Decliner and Faller" toward the then poor girl was thoroughly selfish and unscrupulous.

The rooms are renovated and the place is offered for rent, but nothing is destroyed. The formal park at the side of the château is little changed : along yonder wooded aisle and upon this *allée* between prim patches of sward the de Staël walked with her guests in the summers of long ago ; upon the seat beneath this coppice, beside this placid pool, or on the margin of yonder brooklet from the top of Jura, they lingered in brilliant converse till the stars came out one by one above the darkening mountains. These—the mute, soulless inanimates—remain, while the illustrious company that quickened and glorified them all has vanished from human ken.

Tomb of Necker and de Staël

Some rods distant from the château, shaded by a sombre grove and bounded by a hoary wall, is the picturesque chapel in which Necker is laid with his wife, to whose tomb he, for many years, daily came to pray. In the same crypt the mortal part of de Staël rests at his feet; the portal was walled up at her burial and eye hath not since seen her sepulchre. A stone which marks the grave of her son Auguste, and lies on the threshold of that sealed portal, is fittingly inscribed, "Why seek ye the living among the dead?"

Beyond the closed gate we pause for a parting view of the scene, now flooded with sunshine, and as we leave the place we carry thence that resplendent vision embalmed in a memory that will abide with us forever. As I write these closing lines I see again that summer sky, cloudless save for the fleece floating above Jura like that which the bereaved Necker fancied was bearing the soul of his wife to paradise. I see again the glimmering water; the mountains with their tiaras of snow, sending back the sunbeams from their shining peaks like reflections from the pearly gates that enclose the Celestial City; and, amid this sublime beauty, the gleaming sycamores that sway above the tomb of "the incomparable Corinna."

INDEX

Index

Index

Index

Index

Index

THE END.

LITERARY SHRINES:

THE HAUNTS OF SOME FAMOUS AMERICAN AUTHORS.

By Theo. F. Wolfe, M.D., Ph.D.,

Author of "A Literary Pilgrimage," etc.

Illustrated with four photogravures.

12mo. Crushed buckram, gilt top, deckel edges, $1.25;
half calf or half morocco, $3.00.

CONTAINS, AMONG OTHERS, CHAPTERS TREATING OF

CONCORD: A Village of Literary Shrines.
THE OLD MANSE.
THE HOMES OF EMERSON AND ALCOTT.
HAWTHORNE'S "WAYSIDE."
THE WALDEN OF THOREAU.
IN LITERARY BOSTON.
OUT OF BOSTON: Cambridge—Elmwood—Mt.
Auburn—"Wayside Inn"—Brook Farm—Web-
ster's Marshfield—Homes of Whittier, Haw-
thorne's Salem, etc.
IN BERKSHIRE WITH HAWTHORNE: The
Graylock Region—Middle and Lower Berk-
shire—Haunts of Hawthorne, Thoreau, Bryant,
Melville, Sedgwick, Kemble, Holmes, Long-
fellow, etc.
A DAY WITH THE GOOD GRAY POET.

Uniform with "A Literary Pilgrimage."

J. B. Lippincott Company, Publishers,

PHILADELPHIA.

BY ANNE HOLLINGSWORTH WHARTON.

THROUGH COLONIAL DOORWAYS.

With a number of Colonial Illustrations from Drawings specially made for the work. 12mo. Cloth, $1.25.

"It is a pleasant retrospect of fashionable New York and Philadelphia society during and immediately following the Revolution ; for there was a Four Hundred even in those days, and some of them were Whigs and some were Tories, but all enjoyed feasting and dancing, of which there seemed to be no limit. And this little book tells us about the belles of the Philadelphia meschianza, who they were, how they dressed, and how they flirted with Major André and other officers in Sir William Howe's wicked employ."—*Philadelphia Record.*

COLONIAL DAYS AND DAMES.

With numerous Illustrations. 12mo. Cloth, $1.25.

"In less skilful hands than those of Anne Holllingsworth Wharton's, these scraps of reminiscences from diaries and letters would prove but dry bones. But she has made them so charming that it is as if she had taken dried roses from an old album and freshened them into bloom and perfume. Each slight paragraph from a letter is framed in historical sketches of local affairs or with some account of the people who knew the letter writers, or were at least of their date, and there are pretty suggestions as to how and why such letters were written, with hints of love affairs, which lend a rose-colored veil to what were probably every-day matters in colonial families."—*Pittsburg Bulletin.*

J. B. LIPPINCOTT COMPANY,

PHILADELPHIA.